HOW IT ALL BLEW UP

HOW IT ALL BLEW UP

ARVIN AHMADI

VIKING

VIKING

An imprint of Penguin Random House LLC, New York

First published in the United States of America by Viking,
an imprint of Penguin Random House LLC, 2020

Visit us online at penguinrandomhouse.com

LIBRARY OF CONGRESS CATALOGING-IN-PUBLICATION DATA IS AVAILABLE
ISBN 9780593202876

Printed in the USA   Set in Dante MT Std   Interior design by Jim Hoover

10   9   8   7   6   5   4   3   2   1

For my family

HOW IT ALL BLEW UP

This is a story
based on true events

Interrogation Room 37

Amir

FIRST, LET ME *get one thing straight: I'm not a terrorist. I'm gay. I can see from the look on your face that you're skeptical, and I get it. People like me aren't supposed to exist, let alone make an admission like that in a situation like this. But I assure you, I'm real. I'm here. I'm Iranian. And I'm gay. I just needed to get that off my chest before we started, since you asked why my family and I were fighting on that plane. It had nothing to do with terrorism and everything to do with me.*

Okay, I'll assume from the way you're clearing your throat that I should probably stick to the questions. Sorry, sir. I didn't mean to be disrespectful.

My name is Amir Azadi. I'm eighteen years old.

I was in Rome for about a month. Yes, like Italy. I don't know exactly how many days I was there.

I lived in multiple apartments in Rome. I can get you the addresses if you'd like. My family found me in the Italian countryside yesterday. I willingly went back with them. I can't really say why—it happened so fast—and then we fought on the plane, which is, I guess, why I'm in here.

It was such a huge whirlwind of emotions that I didn't even notice when the flight attendants started pulling the four of us apart. They put us in separate parts of the plane. One of them was actually really kind to me. "Family can take a while," he said as he buckled me into a pull-down seat in the aircraft kitchen. He had an earring in his nose. Slick blond hair. "Trust me, kid, we've all been there." He even let me have one of those snack packs with the hummus and pita chips, which was nice, considering I was being detained.

As soon as we landed, Customs and Border Protection took our passports and escorted us from the plane to a holding room in the airport. Soraya—my little sister—kept asking what was going on, and my mom kept telling her to be quiet.

They told us to sit and wait until our names were called. We were glued to those chairs. Soraya took out her phone and one of the officers barked at her to turn it off. My mom snatched it from her hand. After what felt like forever, one of the male officers entered the room and looked sternly at my dad. "Mr. Azadi. Please come with me." My dad didn't ask any questions. He just went. Then a minute later, I got pulled into this room.

Was I in touch with any "organizations" while I was in Rome? Oh God. You must think I ran away to join ISIS, don't you? You probably think they recruited me to their Italian satellite office. Sir, I don't mean to belittle the evils of the world, but those guys would never take a fruit like me.

I'm sorry we scared all those people on that plane, I really am. I wish I hadn't exploded at my parents like that, all spit and tears and hysteria, on an airplane. Especially being, you know. Of a certain complexion. But at the end of the day, I'd much rather be in this airport interrogation room than back in the closet.

You asked me why we were fighting, sir, and to answer that question, I'll have to start at the very beginning.

Ten Months Ago

IT WAS THE first day of school, and I was already sweating in my seat. As if it wasn't torture enough to sit through transfer orientation, the classroom was as hot as an oven. Figures I move farther south of the Mason-Dixon line and the air conditioner decides to crap out.

The senior class president was fanning himself with a manila folder in the front of the classroom. He was about to introduce us to our "buddies"—student government leaders and athletes, clearly, who would be showing us around the school.

I scanned the lineup.

Not the cute one. Anyone but the cute one.

The one all the way at the end of the row. The one with the messy blond hair and nice arms and golden skin. The one I was too scared to call "cute," even in my head, even though I just did. Right, it should have been: *anyone but the one on the far right, who will make me feel even more sweaty and uncomfortable than I already am.*

The other three senior transfers were all girls, and judging from how they were ogling this dude, they definitely wanted him as their buddy.

I just don't get all the hype around pretty people. I get why they exist—for meet-cute purposes, for magazine spreads—but they're just so stressful to be around. Who needs that kind of stress in their life? Not me.

Not him. Anyone but him.

I imagined the Sorting Hat whispering in my ear: *Not him, eh? Are you sure?* Yes, you pretentious hat, I'm sure. If you can save Harry from Slytherin, you can save me from having to spend the next hour with this annoyingly handsome jock.

Not him, not him, not him . . .

The Sorting Hat did not have my back.

His name was Jackson Preacher. He looked right through me when the president said our names together. When we met, his "hello" was like walking straight into a brick wall. While everyone else's "buddies" enthusiastically asked them questions, Jackson and I just stood there with our hands in our pockets.

He was just as stoic as he took me to my locker, walked me through the main hall and past all the classrooms.

"This is the library," Jackson mumbled when we passed the library, which was marked in big bold letters: LIBRARY. He didn't really have much to say, and I didn't really have much to ask.

What did it matter, anyway? One year at this new high school and I'd be out. That was half the reason why I didn't hate the idea of moving; my dad's new job came with a higher salary, which meant we could afford out-of-state tuition for college. In a year, I'd be somewhere far away. In a year, I could start being myself. That had always been my dream. It was the only reason I didn't fight as hard as my sister about the move.

At the end of the tour, when I assumed Jackson would resume his God-given right as a jock to ignore me for the rest of the school year, he said, "Well, that's it. Let me know if you ever need a hand with anything around here."

I cocked my head back. "Seriously?" He didn't strike me as the hand-offering type. "Is that a real offer?"

Jackson looked off to the side. He shrugged.

"They make you say that, don't they?" I said.

He nodded. "It's part of the script."

"Gotta follow the script," I said, and out of nowhere, Jackson let out one of those snort-laughs. Then we kind of widened our eyes and looked away, because this conversation wasn't part of *our* script.

Jackson combed a hand through his wavy mop of hair. Some days his hair was dirty blond, some days it was brown. I remember that day it was blond.

I asked if he thought I would fit in at this new school. Jackson didn't really answer; he was staring at the parking lot behind me. I had my eyes glued to the school entrance behind him. Later, we would joke that that first day we met, we were actually competing in a very serious un-staring contest.

"It's fine," I said after a long silence. "I don't really fit in any-where."

Jackson smiled—and I cheated at our contest. I snuck a glance at him. Something in him knew. He had found himself another outsider. We fit like gloves, Jackson Preacher and me. We fit like pasta and wine, football and Bud Light.

I was the pasta and wine. He was the football and Bud Light.

That first semester, Jackson and I existed in completely different worlds. As much as we crossed paths, we never really talked. He flew in the stratosphere of athletes and popular kids; I flew under the radar. I just didn't see the point in going through the social acrobatics of making friends when I was only going to be at that school for eight months.

Still, we kept playing our un-staring contest in the halls whenever we passed each other. There was something lingering from that tour, and it was going to take a seismic shift to get it out.

That seismic shift happened right before Thanksgiving, when our football team lost the last game of the season. I was driving home after the game and stopped by 7-Eleven to pick up some salt-and-vinegar chips when I found Jackson sulking in the parking lot. I thought about just walking inside like I didn't see him. But he had dirt marks all over his face. A dried-up river of tears running down his cheeks. He was vulnerable. So I said, "Need a hand?"

He looked up and saw it was me, and he laughed. "I'm supposed to be giving you a hand," Jackson said, wiping a tear from his face.

"Screw the script," I said.

He looked at me differently after those words slid out of my mouth. I don't know what invisible hand gave me the push I needed that night to respond so smoothly, but it will forever go down as the best and worst decision I made in high school.

I comforted Jackson that night, in the grassy corner of the parking lot. I remember his hair was dark and sweaty. I don't know how long we were talking, only that I got to see Jackson in all his multitudes. I saw him, blond and brown-haired, stoic and sensitive, a guy who plays football but who maybe, just maybe, plays for the other team, too.

When I walked him over to his car, he put a hand on my shoulder and squeezed tight. "Remember that thing you were telling me when we met," he said softly, "about not really fitting in anywhere?" My eyes grew wide. I stared right at him, his green eyes, and he was staring back at me. "I feel that way, too."

And right there, the world shifted.

I wish I could just slip back into that little crack in the universe, that guilt-free space where I wanted Jackson Preacher's touch and nothing else. A week later, I was sitting in the passenger seat of his car, fumbling with my sweaty fingers. I was quiet. Jackson was quiet. The radio was humming softly, something poppy. He later told me he kept expecting me to make a move, since, in a way, I had made the first one, but I didn't have any more moves left in me. When he finally put a hand on my shaking leg and leaned in to kiss me, I pulled back. That really scared the shit out of Jackson. He looked like he wanted to die right there. But I needed that second, that frozen moment in time, to say goodbye to my old life. The way you might take one last look at your house after the moving boxes are all packed up. That's all I needed. A second. When I finally pressed my lips against his, I swear, I could feel us both exhaling.

Jackson taught me how to breathe. A special method of breathing that involved drowning, because, boy, was he a slobbery kisser.

I was so happy between Thanksgiving and the middle of March, when I had Jackson and not much else. I should have known Ben and Jake would smell my happiness like a shark smells blood.

Ben and Jake had singled me out from day one at my new school. Much like those "random" security checks at the airport, they picked on me without any probable cause. I was brown, and I was there.

One morning, they deviated from their routine cafeteria traffic stop and caught up with me at my locker. Ben flashed a phone in front of my face.

"We know what you're up to, Jihadi," Jake said, gesturing at the picture on the phone. I took a closer look, and when I made out what it was, I tried to steal the phone from his hand. Jake grabbed my wrist.

It was a picture of Jackson and me kissing in his car.

Ben leaned in closer and went, "You wouldn't want us to smear your faggy little secret across town, would you, Amir Bin Laden? Wouldn't look so great for your people."

Their words stung so hard that I didn't even register that they had followed Jackson and me into the empty parking lot where we hooked up when both our parents were home. I didn't even get a good look at the photo. It's hard looking at a photo like that, at the face of the first boy you've ever kissed, without imagining the creepy stare of the two boys who would blackmail you with the most intimate detail of your life.

"One thousand dollars of your Wiki fortune, and we won't show this shit to your parents," Jake said. He nudged Ben, who nodded. Looking at them, it hit me that they were dead serious: they really did believe I was a "Wiki millionaire."

The thing is, I'm actually very legit in the Wikipedia world, to the point where I actually *do* receive offers to make and edit pages for money. It started in tenth grade, when a friend's mom wanted to hire a Wikipedia editor to make a page for her lingerie start-up. My friend commented on the Facebook post, "Amir!!" and the rest was history. I didn't take the offer, or any of the offers that followed. Paid articles are strictly forbidden in the Wikipedia terms of use. But when Ben and Jake once caught me editing the *Real Housewives of New Jersey* page in homeroom, I didn't think it would hurt to *pretend* I got paid. It's a lot cooler to say "I do this for money" than "I do this because I find the power of crowdsourcing and the democratization of information really sexy."

I didn't have the kind of money they wanted. I begged Ben and Jake to believe me, but they refused. Especially Jake. He was weirdly insistent about the whole thing. It was like he was desperately clinging to this fantasy notion that I was *actually* a Wikipedia millionaire.

It was less of an explosion, and more of a steady crumbling inside of me, when I realized what had just happened.

All the meticulous planning I had put into how I would come out to my parents, the years I spent closeted but knowing I had to come out the *right way*: poof. It was dust in the wind. Ben and

Jake were very clear: if I didn't get them the money in one month, I was fucked.

There was one more condition: "Don't go telling your gay lover about our deal," Ben added. "If anyone finds out about this, this shit's going straight to your parents."

Ben and Jake bulldozed right through the fortress I'd spent years building around my secret.

When you're gay, you grow up doing a lot of mental math. Your brain is basically a big rainbow scoreboard, logging every little thing your parents say—their offhand remarks, the way they react to two men holding hands at the mall or the latest Nike commercial with a queer couple in it. You assign each event a point value. Plus or minus. When the time comes, you tally up all the points—and believe me, you don't forget a single one—and based on the final score, you decide what your coming out is going to look like.

+1: Mom watches Ellen DeGeneres and doesn't bat an eyelash whenever Ellen talks about her wife, Portia.

-1: Mom teaches at the local Islamic school.

-5: When one of her students asks about gay marriage, Mom explains that marriage is between a man and a woman.

-20: The trailer for a gay rom-com comes on while we're at the movie theater, and Dad calls it propaganda.

-2: Mom scrunches up her face at that same trailer.

-1,000,000: We're Muslim.

To be honest: I didn't see a world where my coming out wasn't going to be messy. Pluses and minuses aside, I had bought into the same idea as everyone else, that Muslims and gay people are about as incompatible as Amish people and Apple products. I wish I could say I was better than that, that I ignored the stereotype. But when your safety hinges on a stereotype being true or not, you don't get to be brave. I wasn't going to bet my happiness on the fact that my mom watched a talk show hosted by a lesbian.

But none of that mattered anymore. My happiness hinged on a pair of greedy bastards and their blackmail scheme. I had four weeks and two options: either give in and pay them off, or come out to my parents.

Week one: I was freaking out inside my head. I holed myself up in my room. I stopped texting Jackson. He confronted me in the parking lot one afternoon: "Amir. What's wrong?" I remember staring at the outline of his wide shoulders, the edges of his blond hair, which he refused to cut. I couldn't look at his eyes—it was our un-staring contest all over again—because all I could see in those eyes was that stupid picture of us kissing, flashing before me like a neon sign.

"If something happened, you can tell me," Jackson said, shifting his eyes. It was clear he was nervous to be seen talking to me. Even with all the time we spent together in his car, we still barely talked at school.

"It's nothing, Jackson."

"Is it your parents?" He turned his face away toward the football field, puffing his chest. "If there's something going on, I want to—"

"No, you don't," I snapped. "You don't want to help. I just need space."

Week two: things only got worse. I started hearing back from the colleges I applied to. The rejection letters trickled into my in-box, one after another: NYU, Columbia, Northwestern, Georgetown, Boston College, George Washington. It was like one long, drawn-out funeral, especially around my parents. They got really silent and mostly reacted with sighs and tight-lipped nods. Pretty soon I realized I hadn't just ruined my future; I had ruined their American Dream.

I was angry, too. College was supposed to be my light at the end of the tunnel—when I would be able to come out to my parents safely, with some distance between us. I was counting on one of those schools to be my escape. With the exception of my two safety schools, they all turned me away.

I retreated into my shell. Turned quiet at home. Quiet at school.

By week three, the blackmail was back to being constantly on my mind. I had less than seven days left, and I still had the same two options: come up with the money, or come out. Since I was in no position to disappoint my parents even more, I decided to give in to Ben and Jake's demands. But after I did the dirty deed on Wikipedia and sent them the money, I got a separate text from Jake: he wanted another three thousand dollars, this time by graduation day. That fucker.

I thought about coming out to my parents. I kept pulling up that mental scoreboard, but I just couldn't find a way to make the numbers work. Every time I opened my mouth and tried, I failed.

Every time I thought about pushing it just an inch—testing the waters with a *what if I liked boys?*-type comment—I chickened out. It's hard enough tiptoeing around your entire life with a secret like that. It's draining, constantly feeling that you might not be safe around your own family. My parents were already looking at me differently after I got rejected from all those colleges; if I told them I was gay, I would cease to be their son. I'd become a stranger they had wasted their time raising.

A week before graduation, my family was sitting down for dinner when the phone rang. My mom answered, then handed it to me. "Amir, it's for you."

"*Ameeeer.*" It was Jake. My heart started racing when I heard his wormy voice through the speaker. "I like your mom's accent," he sneered. "So exotic."

I ran up the stairs to my room. Shut the door. My mouth was so dry, I could barely speak. "Why are you calling me?"

"Somehow I don't think your mom would approve of your other life, *Ameer.*" The way Jake said my name, mimicking my mother's accent, it was like he had discovered a new weapon that he could torture me with.

Jake then got to the point, demanding to know when I was going to get him the money. I wanted to be brave and tell him to leave me the hell alone . . . but then I thought about my family downstairs, the peaceful dinner we were having. I collapsed onto my bed, shoving my face into my pillow. All I could think, over and over, was: *I can't do this.*

After that night, I accepted that there was no universe in which

I was capable of coming out. I tried to get the money. I really did. I busted my nerdy ass, reaching back out to every single start-up or D-list celebrity who'd ever slid into my inbox thirsty for a Wikipedia page, but at the end of it all, I was still a thousand bucks short. A couple nights before graduation, I came *this* close to texting Jake to ask if two thousand—two thousand dollars!—would work. But just before I pressed SEND, it came to me. A new idea, a third option I had never considered before.

Disappear. Just for a little while.

I knew the idea was ridiculous. So ridiculous, in fact, that the fantasy of skipping graduation and going somewhere else was actually comforting for about five seconds. It was the calmest I had felt in months.

Then I kept thinking. And the more I thought about it, just completely removing myself from this entire mess until things calmed down, the less ridiculous it seemed. You don't just stand aside when a bomb is about to detonate. You run.

The morning of graduation, I was hyperventilating in my car in the driveway, a packed duffel bag on the passenger seat next to me. *This is it*, I kept thinking. I couldn't believe I was following through on this insane idea. But in a few hours, Jake was going to spill my secret to my parents in the middle of graduation. He'd already told me as much the day before at school.

I, however, would be on a plane thousands of feet in the air. I would be safe. I would have space. And when I landed, I would have the most important answer of my life: I would know if my family still loved me or not. If they did, then I would come home.

And if they didn't—well, I would be far away, just as I'd always planned.

When I finally started driving, I felt the clash of my two identities stronger than ever. Iranian. Gay. There had always been a wall separating those two sides of me, so they would never touch. On one side, there was Jackson. On the other, my family. Soon, that wall would come crashing down.

I let out a deep sigh. And then I watched through the rearview mirror as my house shrank smaller and smaller, until it disappeared.

Interrogation Room 37

Amir

THAT WAS THE *original plan. I just wanted to go to New York. NYU and Columbia were two of my dream schools, and I thought I would get away while Jake hijacked my coming out. You have to understand that I was imagining the worst, and if my parents didn't want me back home, then I would create a new life for myself in New York.*

Rome was never part of the original plan.

Have I been in touch with Jackson since I left America? Yes and no. It's complicated. I can't believe I'm about to say this to you in here, but I keep wondering if I loved Jackson. I don't know. We tiptoed around that word a lot. We tiptoed around a lot of things. All I know is that neither of us ever believed we would end up together. We didn't believe in a future for "us" as much as we believed in a future where, someday, I could be Amir . . . and he could be himself, too.

You're looking at me like none of this is relevant to the outburst on the plane, but it is. It's the baggage. I thought you people were all about inspecting baggage.

Sorry, I shouldn't have said that. I was just trying to emphasize, with my long-winded story, that it really all comes back to Jackson. If I'd never met Jackson, I wouldn't be in here. I can draw a clear line connecting that first moment we kissed to right now, sitting in this chair, absolutely terrified to see the people on the other side of this wall. More terrified to talk to them than to you, if I'm being honest.

Interrogation Room 38

Soraya

MY NAME IS *Soraya Azadi. I'm thirteen years old.*

My brother, Amir, has been missing for a month. He disappeared the morning of his high school graduation.

Did I notice anything different or off about Amir before he disappeared? Was he talking to anyone suspicious? Well—

Mom, don't give me that look. Amir is in the room next door, and I'm sure he's telling the truth. He has nothing to be ashamed of. I'm sorry, Officer. I didn't mean to snap. I'm just a little annoyed, that's all. I don't think it's fair how my family got pulled into these rooms. I really don't think it's fair. I tried to record the whole thing back in the waiting room, but my mom made me put my phone away.

It has been a big misunderstanding. I'm so glad you can see that.

Sure. I can tell you everything. How long do you think this is going to take? I've already missed two rehearsals for the summer musical, and if I miss tonight's, I . . . My mom is giving me that look again. She thinks I'm saying too much. It's funny, I knew she would be like this when you asked to talk to me first. You see her face, right? I'll read it for you: Soraya, be careful what you say. Soraya, we are Iranian. We deal with these matters privately, Soraya. *If she were answering your question, she'd say no, we didn't notice any signs that Amir was going to run away. And she'd be telling the truth. From her perspective, nothing was wrong. Nothing is ever wrong in her mind.*

No, Mom, let me talk! What her face should be saying is, Soraya, thank you. Soraya, you saved the day. Soraya, it's because of you we found your brother and brought him back.

Let me explain.

Interrogation Room 39

Afshin Azadi

BEFORE WE GO *any further, let me get this straight. You are questioning my son in one room, correct? And my daughter and wife are together in another room. And you have me alone here in this room—and I think I know why you have put me in this separate room. I know it in my bones. The way you are looking at me, I think you know, too. That this is not my first time alone in a small room, just like this one.*

Very well.

No, I don't have anything more to say.

Thirty-One Days Ago

WHEN I LANDED at JFK Airport, the morning of my graduation, I felt safe. I was a world away from the nightmare of my senior spring. Most of all, I was away from Jake and the trouble he was about to cause for my family.

I made myself check my phone. Graduation would be over by now. I imagined this whole scenario like I had thrown a grenade, sprinted away, and now I was looking back to see if it had actually exploded, or if it was a dud.

I sat there in my cramped airplane seat. I wasn't even connected to the cell network yet. I shook my phone. Held it up in the air.

Finally, the bars popped up in the corner of my phone screen. I had service. And there they were: fifteen texts, all from my mother, father, and sister. I checked my call log. Five new voicemails. I went back to the texts and started reading. *Amir, where are you? Amir, is everything all right? Amir, why aren't you answering your phone? Amir why aren't you home? Where have you gone? Please answer and tell us you're all right.*

I texted back immediately. *I'm fine. I can explain.* And then I held my breath. Because at this point, my family knew. They had to know. Last week, Jake had made it very clear that if I didn't get him the money, he would out me during the ceremony. He had even suggested texting the picture to my parents before they started reading out names. The thought of walking across that stage, hearing silence from where my mom, dad, and sister were sitting—it had made me want to throw up.

My phone buzzed. It was Mom: *Good. We love you.*

I must have stared at the text for a solid minute before looking back up and around the plane. All the other passengers had deplaned.

My heart rate slowed down as I took in the words.

My family still loved me.

I took my duffel bag from the overhead compartment and held it close to my chest. All spring, I had wondered how they would react to Jake's news. Would they think he was lying? Would they tell themselves that it was photoshopped?

Whatever they believed—they loved me.

I felt giddy as I shuffled off the plane. I thought about the rainbow scoreboard, all the positives that I had clearly discounted. I thought about how my parents had in fact raised me to treat people equally, how they didn't subscribe to every single little piece of our religion and culture. They were complicated. They could surprise me. I should have expected better of them.

When I was finally off the plane, I called them back.

"Amir?" my mom said frantically. "Oh, Amir. We were worried sick!"

"What were you thinking?" my dad chimed in. "Where were you?"

"I'm sorry, I'm sorry. I can explain." I was walking down the long hall of the airport, past Cinnabon and Hudson News. "I was just scared . . ."

"Scared of what?" my dad asked.

My heart skipped a beat. I stood outside the smelly airport bathroom, between the men's and women's bathrooms. I was confused. "Are you still at graduation?" I asked.

"No. We looked for you after the ceremony, but you weren't there."

I considered my next words carefully. "Did you talk to any of my classmates . . ."

"We asked some of them if they knew where you were," my dad said. "*Joonam, azizam*, what's wrong?"

My life, my dear. Whenever I got upset, my dad went overkill with Persian terms of endearment.

"What happened?" I heard my sister pipe up in the background.

"Where are you, Amir?" my mom asked.

I was freaking out. My mom and dad sounded so genuinely concerned over the phone. They sounded like they loved me. It made me feel like even more of a fraud.

An announcement blared overhead: "Welcome to New York-Kennedy International Airport . . ."

My mom and dad started talking all at once, interrupting each other. "Amir, are you at an airport?" "Amir, are you in New York?" "Amir, what's wrong?" Amir, Amir, Amir . . .

I hung up the phone.

I stood there, motionless, in the middle of the bustling airport. Jake hadn't told them. He'd backed out.

Someone's suitcase bumped into my leg then, so I moved. I wandered aimlessly around the airport. I had no idea what to do. I felt lost, with my duffel and all the sounds. The people around me. I realized I still had my earbuds in.

My plan had backfired.

I couldn't go back home. If I did, I'd have to explain to my parents why I had run away and deal with the ensuing explosion in person. And even if I did manage to come up with an excuse for why I'd skipped my own graduation, Jake would still be holding my secret over me. Maybe he hadn't backed out, after all. Maybe he had instead figured out a way to level up his blackmail.

I found a bathroom and went into a stall. (I've watched enough teen movies to know that this is the best place to deal with life crises.) I checked my phone again and saw that Jackson had texted me. So had my friends from Maryland. My mom must have gotten in touch with them.

Today's choose-your-own-fucked-up-adventure was supposed to go down one of two ways. If my parents told me they accepted me as gay, I'd come right back home. If they didn't, I would start a new life. But what was I supposed to do *now*?

I stumbled out of the bathroom and nearly smacked headlong into one of those glowing departures boards. I stared up at the endless list of cities.

Why was I so afraid of going home? Why couldn't I be brave, march right up to my parents and tell them what had happened, the reason I wasn't at my own graduation? Why couldn't I come out to them? Why couldn't I just say the words?

My eyes flickered around the list of cities. Chicago. San Francisco. Atlanta. Each one was an invitation, an escape hatch, a safe haven.

My phone was buzzing. It had been buzzing the entire time, I realized, like I had a vibrator strapped onto my thigh. But I couldn't pick up. I just couldn't. But I also couldn't stay in New York; my parents knew that I was here. They could find me here.

I had to go somewhere else. Chicago. San Francisco. Atlanta.

I ran my hands over my jean pockets and felt the outline of my passport. Why had I brought my passport? I don't know. Maybe some part of me, when I imagined the possibility that I might not go back home, saw this as some kind of national emergency, one where I might even need to flee the country? Crazy, I know.

On the other hand, looking at the list of possible destinations, it didn't seem so crazy now. I had my Wiki money. I could go anywhere. And why not somewhere outside America? London. Paris. Barcelona.

That was when I looked to the right of the departures sign and saw a gelato shop. Bright, heavenly lighting, and an array of the most colorful ice cream flavors I'd ever seen in my life. I stepped toward the light to better inspect the rainbow colors, the strawberry reds, the chocolates and vanillas.

Now that I think of it, it's wild how a gelato shop can change the literal course of your life.

Interrogation Room 38

Roya Azadi

BEFORE WE GO *further, ma'am, please allow me to apologize for my son's startling behavior on that airplane today. I assure you it was completely out of the ordinary for him, and nothing to worry about— just a private family matter. And please allow me to apologize for my daughter. I understand why you want to speak with her, and I appreciate that you've allowed me to be in the room during your questioning. But she has been very emotional this past month, with her brother gone. Haven't you, Soraya? Look, she's rolling her eyes now because she doesn't like it when I put words in her mouth. What teenage girl does?*

My purse? Yes, of course you may have a look. Here.

Those are all hand sanitizer bottles. I assure you, they are less than— oh, no, that one is, yes, that one is more than three ounces. I am so sorry. It was on sale at CVS, and I wasn't thinking . . .

That is my phone. You need my password? Of course. Soraya, please, calm down. It's fine.

That is a picture of me with my students. I posted it on Instagram at the end of the school year. I teach at a Farsi school, and when I teach, I wear the hijab. You see, I am not wearing it now, but the class takes place at a mosque, so I wear it then.

That—that is my friend Maryam's Instagram page. Those are Quran verses. She is quite devout. I do not see how this is relevant to—um, yes. I, I understand the verse. It is about finding your path when you are lost. It is quite peaceful, I assure you. Though it is in Arabic, not Farsi. Officer, Islam, like any religion, is very complex, and people practice it in many different ways, and I hope you don't—

I understand you have to do your job and ask questions. Absolutely. I completely understand. And I appreciate your patience with us, with my husband—I understand your colleagues needed to question him separately, because of a past issue. We are more than happy to answer whatever questions you have. But please know that what happened on the plane, it is a sensitive matter, a delicate issue that we are still working through as a family. Soraya was correct earlier, when she assumed what I would have wanted to say. In our culture, these matters are usually dealt with privately.

That? It is a picture I took at Amir's graduation ceremony, when we first discovered that he was missing. We got to the auditorium early, to get good seats—we had very good seats, in the third row on the right side of the stage.

I first noticed Amir was missing when I saw he wasn't seated in the front row. He should have been in the front row—according to the program, seating was alphabetical. Amir Azadi. Soraya and my husband both said it had to be some kind of mistake, that he must have gotten seated somewhere in the sea of other kids, but I knew something was wrong. Blame it on my maternal instinct. I'd lost my son one time before, at Disney World, and I felt the same stomach-churning I had felt then. He had wandered off back then, Amir, on some kind of necessary adventure. When we found him, he was in a minor brawl with Goofy. He had really angered the man in the Goofy costume; apparently, Amir had punched him in the nose. He was only five. It was a misunderstanding.

I looked for Amir in the crowd of students. I looked for his face in the ocean of red caps and gowns. Nothing.

I texted Amir. Many times. Outside the auditorium, we were surrounded by caps and gowns, all the families snapping photos like paparazzi. It hadn't hit me yet that we wouldn't get to take photos like that with our son.

During the ceremony, a tall, wiry boy kept looking our way. He would approach us and then back away, almost like he wanted to talk to us. He had very messy hair. I remember thinking, This boy's mother needs to get him to a barber. He had looked quite nervous.

Maybe you should talk to him, Officer?

Interrogation Room 38

Soraya

FU—FREAKING JAKE. *I'm sorry. I don't usually cuss. But if I'd known who he was that day, I would have kicked him right in the balls. Yes, Mom, that was Jake. And I hate him even more now, knowing that he almost talked to us on graduation day.*

Amir didn't have any friends at his new school, as far as we knew, so we called Lexa and Arun, his best friends from Maryland, to see if they'd heard from him. They told us Amir hadn't contacted them. In fact, they said he'd gone kind of radio silent on them after Thanksgiving, right when Amir started—well, I'll get to that. Apparently, they had tried reaching out to Amir a few weeks before graduation. They hadn't heard anything from him about college, and they remembered how much he always wanted to go to college in New York. They said it was an awkward FaceTime call. Amir was moody. They said he didn't really want to talk about his future at all.

That really worried my parents. We checked his room and there was nothing. No note. But then Mom went and checked his drawers, and she noticed a bunch of underwear and shirts were missing. He'd gone some-

where. We called his cell phone, but it kept going straight to voicemail. That really worried my parents. Where had he gone?

When he finally called us back, my parents were so freaking relieved. It was like someone told them they had won a million dollars. I'm not kidding: my mom actually jumped and clapped her hands when she heard the caller ID. But then they found out Amir was at the airport, and he just weirdly hung up on us. My dad got really quiet. I could tell he was thinking about the last time Amir had run away from home—two years ago. "Damn it," he said abruptly. "What did I say this time?" Then he looked at me and smiled. "Don't worry, joonam. Your brother will come home."

The house was so quiet that first night without Amir. It was dark, empty, dead. When I was little, I always imagined death like walking in the dark. I know, I was so dramatic back then, I was such a baby. You remember, Mom? When I would run into your bedroom and sleep between you and Dad because I was scared? For the record, I don't do that anymore, Officer.

The next morning, I asked my parents if they were going to call the police so they could look for Amir. We had all gotten up early, when it was barely light outside. My mom and dad were standing against the stovetop with their crystal tea glasses. They looked at me with these fake smiles and told me not to worry.

No, Mom, that's exactly what you said. In your fantasy world, Amir was going to come home on his own, just like the last time. And then, in your fantasy world, you would bury whatever issue he had under the Persian rug. Again.

But I know my brother. He hadn't been happy for a while. And this time was different.

The house felt dead at night and broken during the day. I would eat my Cheerios at the breakfast table, and Amir wasn't there to tell me to hurry up before they got soggy. My friend Madison would come over, and I couldn't laugh at her jokes. One time, I had to run into the bathroom just to breathe. It was the third or fourth day after Amir left. I just leaned my head against the medicine cabinet and—please don't be mad, Mom, but I thought maybe I would run away myself. Home just didn't feel like home without Amir.

I thought about my favorite book, From the Mixed-Up Files of Mrs. Basil E. Frankweiler. You've read it with your daughter, ma'am? That's so cool. It made me wonder: if Amir really did run away, why didn't he take me with him—like Claudia and Jamie? We had always been pretty close. I couldn't imagine the Amir I knew leaving his little sister without saying goodbye. Unless he had a really good reason to leave.

I needed to figure out that reason. That's when I put on my detective hat. Step one: I started talking to the people in his life.

Interrogation Room 37

Amir

ALL RIGHT: I'VE *given you all the details you asked for—flight number, time, the address where I stayed in Rome. I've shown you the Expedia flight confirmation, the Airbnb receipt, the receipt for the euros I took out at currency exchange, even the picture of the New York City skyline I took from my plane seat. But I'm serious: this trip happened because of gelato. It came together at the last minute, at JFK, and the sole reason I decided on Rome is because I happened upon the sweetest form of ice cream. There were no terrorists. No friends. Just ice cream.*

Thirty Days Ago

THE NEXT THING I knew, I was sitting in the middle of a tiny attic apartment I had booked at the last minute. A literal closet. (The irony was not lost on me.) That was when the sum total of my last twenty-four hours of traveling finally started thudding against my head.

It started lightly and then knocked harder and harder as I stared outside my tiny window at the slant of the rooftop. I let my eyes follow the red tile, down the white building walls, the clay windowsills, all the way to the courtyard, where there was a sexy red Vespa sitting on a bed of cracked brick.

And then, a full-on thwack: Holy shit. I was in *Rome*. They say stress makes you do crazy things. And I mean, I basically blacked out and booked an international trip. That's like the time I fell asleep on the NYC subway and ended up in Harlem, but on a *plane*. I don't remember going to the international departures gate; I don't remember the flight; I don't remember the bus ride into Rome or fitting the key in the hole or taking off my shoes.

I rushed outside, onto the street. There I was: Via della Gensola. Moss-covered walls. Cobble. A couple whizzed by on a Vespa, and my gaze turned with them as they stopped at the end of the street and made out for a few seconds before disappearing into the restaurant. It was the most Italian thing ever.

I ran back to my apartment. I burst into the tiny bathroom, nearly bulldozing the ancient water heating system, and stared at my face in the mirror. Bloodshot eyes. Dark bags underneath them.

Looking at myself, there, I knew: *You've gone too far this time, Amir.*

Through my tiny window, I watched it get dark outside. I listened to the clanging of pots and pans from somewhere down below. I heard bells chiming. I smelled fried onion and garlic rising up. There was something freeing about being thousands of miles away from my problems. It didn't erase them completely, but the distance helped. It always does.

I decided I owed my parents at least the bare minimum of an explanation. So I emailed them: *Mom and Dad, please don't hate me. I'm dealing with a lot right now, but I want you to know that I'm safe. I promise I'm safe, and I'm fine. I just needed to get away for a couple of days.* I closed out of my inbox as soon as I hit SEND.

I woke up the next morning to the smell of fresh bread and frying eggs drifting in my open window. There were still pots and pans banging, but also birds chirping. And sunlight. Glorious, glorious sunlight. I smiled for the first time in days. And I had my first clear thought: *What's a kid like me supposed to do after making the*

craziest decision of his life, when his life is hanging by a thread? How do
you go back to normal after that?

Gelato. I stepped outside and found a little street-side gelato stand, where I splurged and ordered two heaping scoops: one chocolate, one strawberry. The cool sweetness calmed my nerves. The ground below me felt stable again.

The gelato melted quickly as I strolled the colorful streets of Trastevere. There was something magical about this neighborhood, its old doorways and passageways, the young people sitting in plastic chairs outside bars and restaurants, smoking and having coffee without a worry in the world. I took the last bite of my cone, wiped my fingers on my pant legs, and smiled. I liked it here.

I found a bookstore and stepped inside. It was completely empty and air-conditioned. A man yelled "ciao" from the back room; I yelled "ciao" back. I found the English section, and I was flipping through the latest John Green novel when another customer entered the store. She seemed to know the bookseller. I eavesdropped on their conversation. I was surprised that they were not only speaking in English, but the bookseller had a perfect American accent. He asked the woman how her writing was going—she was an Italian author of sexy romance novels. She asked him how his partner was doing.

My ears perked up at the word "partner."

Was the bookseller gay? It could have been his business partner. It could have been his long-term girlfriend. But for some reason, the possibility that this man might be just like me made me happier than I had felt in a long time.

It struck me right there, as I pretended to flip through a copy of *Turtles All the Way Down*, that at any other point in my thus-far-short life, I would have clammed up in this situation. I would have died just being near another gay person, or hearing the word "partner." Whenever my family passed two men holding hands, I felt that if I glanced for just a second too long, I would be exposed. That my mom or dad would figure it out. For once, I didn't have to worry. Not only that, but I had the luxury of feeling like I was a part of something. That word, "partner": that world of men holding hands. It wasn't a threat anymore. It wasn't going to give me away.

Look, I hadn't gotten to steer my own destiny in a very long time. I had been closeted by circumstance. I had been driven to Rome by circumstance. But now that I was here, my circumstances belonged to me. So I decided to do something; I would talk to this man. I would strike up a conversation with him—gay or no—and ask him what to do during my brief time in Rome.

I pretended to flip through a few more books before I heard the door jingle, signaling that the author had left. I finally grabbed a copy of *The Perks of Being a Wallflower* (it was a euro cheaper than the other YA paperbacks) and took it to the checkout desk. The bookstore clerk looked up and dog-eared his page in the book he was reading.

That's when I lost any semblance of cool.

No one should be allowed to look *that* good and work in a bookstore.

Seriously, this guy looked like he had jumped straight off of a romance novel cover. His eyes were absurdly piercing. I wanted to roll a marble down his slicked-back hair. And the way he wore his tank top, light and loose, with tattoos and muscles peeking out from underneath it—they stopped me so hard in my tracks I said a little prayer for all the men and women who had fallen before me.

He was immediately friendly. All, *"Perks!* Wow. Great pick. I haven't read that one in forever."

And I was immediately a fool. Awkward. Clumsy.

The man rang me up and handed me my receipt, and he was prepared to send me off like any other customer, when I blurted, "I'm only in town for a couple days, and I was kind of wondering what there is to do . . . in town?"

He smiled, like any friendly person would, and I think my shoulders actually melted into my chest. He ripped a piece of paper off a notebook to the left of his desk (sadly, that was the only thing he ripped off) and started writing.

"I assume you don't want the tourist traps, like the Colosseum and the Sistine Chapel . . . not that they're not historically important! But you can find those recommended in any guidebook . . . Oh! There's this gorgeous park, Giardino degli Aranci, which is lovely in and of itself, but if you go, you have to find the keyhole. It has the most jaw-dropping view of Rome. Like, you get the most incredible view of Saint Peter's Basilica through it."

He also wrote down a couple of bar and restaurant recommendations.

"Are you old enough to drink?" he asked.

"I don't . . . know," I said. What I started to say was *I don't drink*, but that wasn't true. Not after senior year.

"The drinking age here is eighteen," the book clerk said, twirling his pen on his finger, and in that moment, he was a magician. He was straight-up Cedric Diggory. "I can't believe it's still twenty-one in the States."

I used to genuinely think I'd never drink alcohol. Neither of my parents drink, and I have relatives who call alcohol poison, so it seemed straightforward to me. But Jackson had changed my mind on drinking, among other things.

"In that case, I'm old enough," I told the bookseller.

He started to write something else but scribbled it out. "If only you were staying a bit longer," he said. "My partner just opened a bar—well, not a bar, a cultural association—and the official opening is in a couple of days . . ."

And here I blurted, "Your partner!" like the fool that I am.

He gave me this sideways look and went, "Yes . . ."

And then he wrote down another spot and asked if I've heard of Pigneto—"It's like the Bushwick of Rome"—and I told him I don't even know the Bushwick of wherever-Bushwick-is, and he laughed. Then he wrote a third spot, and a name. "Jahan. That's the name of the bartender there. He's an incredible poet, too."

Suddenly, a shard of sun sliced the bookstore clerk's hair, turning it from brown to blond, and once again, my mind flashed to Jackson. I thought about the texts he'd sent me yesterday—*where are you, what the hell Amir, answer me damn it, are you okay, should I call your parents—*

NO, don't, I finally replied, *I'm fine, family emergency.*

And just like that, all my troubles came flooding back.

I quickly said thanks to this gorgeous bookseller (whose name I didn't even catch) and went on my way.

Outside, the streets were busy and crowded. I came to a four-way intersection and froze. My heart was beating out of my chest, and it was like this entire ancient city—its Colosseum, its Sistine Chapel—had come crashing down over my head.

My thoughts swirled between the bookstore clerk, his slick brown hair, and Jackson, whose hair was getting longer and blonder every day. From Jake, who still owned my secret, to my parents, who still didn't know. At least, I thought they didn't. Who knew what could be happening in my absence?

I swallowed the tightness in my chest long enough to find my way back to the Airbnb. I drank some water and lay down in bed for a couple hours. Then I moved to the floor. I rested the back of my hand over my burning forehead and closed my eyes.

Interrogation Room 39

Afshin Azadi

THIS IS ABSURD. *You've been questioning me nonstop about my background. I've already told you. I was detained once before, just like this. It was ten years ago. Why do I look different from that photo? Because!*

Because I shaved off the beard.

The whole experience frightened me. When you people went through my things and made me feel like a bad guy. I was merely traveling for a work trip. I was carrying a briefcase with chemicals I needed for a convention in Texas, and I believe the intention of my trip was simply . . . misinterpreted.

We never told my children about this, no. They don't know. We didn't want to scare them.

Interrogation Room 37

Amir

I WOULD ABSOLUTELY *love a glass of water, yes. You know, sir, you're not nearly as intimidating as I would have expected you to be. Which is kind of messed up, when you think about it.*

Twenty-Nine Days Ago

I MUST HAVE drunk half the water out of the Tiber River after my panic attack in the bookstore.

The bed in my Airbnb was lofted up by some weird chains that rattled every time I went down the creaky wooden stairs. It also meant that I had to duck my head whenever I went into the kitchen to fill up my glass.

I wanted to go home. My real home. I wanted to be back in my room, with my stupid participation ribbons and the ukulele that Soraya played more than I did. But I couldn't. That was the same room was where I had spent these last couple of months, miserable and depressed. It was the room where I had spent entire weekends with my door shut, scrolling through internet forums that were supposed to help me feel better but only made me feel worse. There are a lot of bad coming-out stories on the internet. I shouldn't have read them all, but I did.

Going home wasn't an option.

Then I remembered the hot bookseller's list of recommendations, crumpled in my pocket. I unfolded it, smoothed the edges, and saw the bartender's name he had written down. Jahan. It was an Iranian name, meaning "world" in Farsi. What were the odds?

So, just before midnight, I decided to leave the apartment and check out this bar. I was more than a little nervous to be out alone in a foreign country. But it was too good of a coincidence, this Iranian bartender in Rome, and besides, a real drink at a real bar sounded like an upgrade from the warm beer Jackson kept in his glove compartment.

It had gotten dark outside, but the streets of Rome still flaunted their effortless beauty. Like, they weren't trying hard at all. The buildings were all worn and painted over in perfect creams and pastels, illuminated by the streetlights, and laundry hung outside the windows, wide sheets and shirts and bright little dresses. The colors all worked together in such a way that it felt like they were a part of the fabric of the neighborhood. And the streets themselves—yes, the cobblestones were uneven, but I was figuring out how to walk on them.

The bar was on a small, dark side street, where you had to ring a doorbell to get inside. Sitting at the bar, there were two women with short-cropped hair; one of them had a huge sunflower tattoo on her bare arm. And behind the bar was a short guy with a big smile and even bigger drunk eyes. Not the kind that were *actually* drunk—he seemed to be pretty composed, balancing two bottles and a shot glass—but the kind that were always a little red and had bags under them. The cute kind.

"I'm looking for Jahan," I told the bartender.

"That's me," he said.

I looked at him again. Was this man messing with me? I don't know how else to say it, but this man did not look like any other Iranian person I had ever met in my life. I mean, his name was more Iranian than kabob and Persepolis. But his skin was covered in tattoos. And quite a few shades darker than mine. Burnt caramel, versus my milkier caramel.

He finished the drink he was making and handed it to the sunflower tattoo lady. *"Jah-han.* You even pronounced it right. The Italians always manage to bastardize my name. You must be Persian. Are you Persian?"

"I am," I said.

"I knew it! I knew it when you walked in. What's your name?"

"Amir."

"Amir," Jahan repeated. *"Befarmah*, welcome. Take a seat. What would you like to drink?"

I sat at one of the tall barstools, my feet dangling above the ground, and rested my elbows on the wet bar. "A beer?"

"What kind of beer?"

I glanced up at the ceiling. "Oh, I'll drink anything."

Jahan gave me a funny look. He could definitely tell I had never ordered a beer in my life.

"One *beer*, coming up. So how did you find us?"

"I was at this bookstore earlier today," I said, "and the bookseller recommended this bar. Well, specifically he recommended you."

"You met Neil! Oh, I love Neil," Jahan said. "He's the sweetest person in the world."

"Jesus Christ, he's *friendly*, too?"

Jahan laughed and filled up a tall beer glass for me. "Congratulations. You have eyes," he said.

I felt embarrassed, knowing that Jahan had figured out that I found Neil attractive, and I took a long sip of my drink. I was pleasantly surprised by how nice it tasted compared to the warm PBRs in Jackson's car.

Jahan kept tending the bar, humming along to the song that was playing overhead.

"What song is this?" I asked.

He looked at me like I came from Mars. "You don't know Nina Simone?"

"That's the name of the song?"

Jahan's jaw dropped. He turned to the two women at the bar and threw his hands up. "Hopeless! This boy is hopeless! Either he's under twenty-five or a flaming heterosexual."

My ears turned red, and my natural instinct was to brush off the comment. I mean, my whole life, even the tiniest gay joke could dig under my skin and make me feel self-conscious. But then I realized I didn't have to brush off Jahan's joke. It didn't have to be awkward. So I replied, "Sorry, but I'm only one of those things."

Jahan grinned so wide you could actually hear it, the soft smacking of spread lips and caved dimples.

"So, where are the Italian people in Rome?" I asked. "Between you and Neil, I've only met other Americans."

"With the state of the economy, they all seem to be fleeing. Young people can't get jobs, there's a rising far-right movement—but hey, at least we still have pasta." Jahan sighed. "Don't get me wrong. Italy is a lovely place to visit, but you've got to be out of your mind to want to live here."

I expected this to be Jahan's cue to move on to his other customers at the bar, and he did—there were beers to pour, fancy drinks to mix—but Jahan also kept doing the most wonderful thing: he'd pull me into his conversations. "You'll have to check that out while you're in town, Amir," he said after telling one tourist about the Sistine Chapel. "Oh, in America, they hurry you out of the restaurant," he said about the slower service in Italy, winking at me. "Our people, they've been around for a long-ass time," he bragged, comparing the Persian Empire to the European monarchies.

It turned out Jahan was just half Iranian, on his dad's side—his mom was Dominican—but after he had had a few drinks himself, all he wanted to talk about with me was Iranian culture.

"Have you heard of Fereydoon? He's this singer," Jahan said. "I'm obsessed with him. He was huge in the 1960s, and he had an emo poet sister, kind of like the Iranian Virginia Woolf. He was also deeply, deeply homosexual. Everyone knew! But of course you couldn't say anything." And then Jahan got up on the bar—I'm serious!—and he performed a bit from one of his songs, flamboyantly flashing his fingers and kicking his legs, and I just thought, *Who is this guy?*

The whole night, Jahan told story after story. His nipple story was particularly gruesome—in the best way.

But before we got really drunk and heard the nipple story told 'round the world—from what I understand, that story has spread farther from its initial source than influenza in 1918 or herpes in a frat house—we listened to Joni Mitchell.

"Do you know this song, Amir?" Jahan asked, leaning over the bar.

I definitely recognized the upbeat melody, the lyrics—paved paradise, something about parking lots—but I didn't know the singer.

"You're hopeless," Jahan said. "Gay card revoked."

It was like there was another rainbow scoreboard for gay men that I had never been exposed to, and I was starting from scratch.

-5: Doesn't know Nina Simone or Joni Mitchell.

"You know, Joni Mitchell is how I came out to my dad," Jahan said.

"Um."

"You don't have to look so horrified." He laughed. "It didn't go *that* badly. I was in the eighth grade, and my dad asked at the dinner table if I had any crushes, and I replied, totally seriously: 'Father. Joni Mitchell is the only woman for me.' The man looked at me, utterly disappointed, shaking his head—but he knew. That was all I ever had to say."

I couldn't believe how nonchalant Jahan was about coming out to his dad. I looked over his face carefully, but I didn't find an ounce of pain, regret, shame, any of the feelings I'd been dealing with these last few months. It was just another story for him, and he went about washing glasses in the bar sink.

"Aladdin," I said quietly.

"What?"

I looked up from my beer.

"It was Aladdin for me."

Jahan placed a clean glass on the dish rack and smiled. "How very on-brand."

I stared in awe as he intercepted a different conversation, this one about a record store in Naples that was run by the Italian mafia. The way Jahan told his tales, with so much flair, they reminded me of the stories my mom and dad had told me growing up. The ones their parents had told them. It felt like part of a thousand-year-old tradition I never thought I would be allowed to be a part of.

The bar emptied out around four in the morning, and I stuck around for another hour. I had been nursing the same beer since midnight, so Jahan made me finish and we took shots of fancy liqueurs. Not liquor. Liqueur. I'd never even heard the word before tonight. I definitely couldn't spell it. Jahan kept making me try.

"L-I-Q-O—"

"Wrong!" he yelled. Another shot.

"L-I-Q-U . . . O—"

"*Wrong!*" he said again, giddily. Another shot.

"I shouldn't be allowed to take shots of this stuff if I can't spell the word," I slurred.

"I don't make the rules," Jahan said.

We left the bar at five in the morning. It hit me as I watched Jahan twisting the key in the rusted padlock that if I was back home, I would have been alone in my room, feeling—what was the opposite of drunk? Sober. I would have been so sober.

There wasn't a single other person on the street outside the bar as we walked. But the way it was lit—warmly, oozing orange and yellow, extending an invitation to any and all—I felt more alive than ever. There was something tugging at my chest, like I'd been accepted into a special secret society.

Jahan asked where I was staying, and I suddenly sobered up, remembering I would have to check out of my Airbnb later that day. I told him where it was, expecting Jahan to point me in the right direction. But it turned out Jahan lived just around the corner. He offered to walk me back. I smiled. After a shitty past couple of days—months, really—I was so happy the universe had at least given me this little bit of serendipity.

We took the long way home, because Jahan wanted to show me Piazza Santa Maria, the main square in our neighborhood, Trastevere. It was massive and inspiring, with a few stragglers humming around the bursting fountain in the middle. "The sound of that fountain always reminds me of children laughing," Jahan said. And the way he said it, with his eyes ambling to the side, just over the tip of the church—it wasn't a story. It wasn't meant to entertain. It was just Jahan.

We looped around the piazza, back to the main road that crossed the Viale, a sort of mini-highway. I started tightrope-walking along the grooves of the tram rails, and Jahan looked at me and laughed. "How old are you, Amir?" he asked.

"Old enough to be in Rome by myself," I said.

"Fair enough," he replied. "Though, to be honest, I thought you were on a family trip and had snuck out for the night. It's what I would have done."

I stumbled off the tram rails, and Jahan jumped on. "And what are you doing in Rome?" he asked.

"Writing," I said, because it seemed as good a bullshit answer as any. Though in a way I was figuratively rewriting my life. I mean, who isn't a writer in the figurative sense of the word?

Jahan chided me for being a writer who doesn't know Joni Mitchell and therefore a disgrace to our entire species. I remembered that he was an actual writer, a poet. Neil had told me just earlier that day.

"Oh, you can't trust anything that man says. He's sick," Jahan said. "Sick in love. His boyfriend, Francesco, is proposing to him in two weeks, on his thirtieth birthday." He winked at me then, and I felt that in trusting me with that secret, he was inviting me deeper into this secret society of Americans in Rome. "If you insist on assigning labels, then yes, I'm a poet," he said. "But I'm a procrastinator, too, so that should tell you how much poetry I actually write."

He dropped me off at my door with a stern warning: "Listen to Joni Mitchell. There will be a quiz next time."

I smiled, because all night, Jahan had been so incredulous about every "icon" I'd never heard of: Joni Mitchell, Nina Simone, Joan Crawford. It was like I had told him I'd never heard of oxygen. I was smiling all the way until I reached the chain staircase to my bed, when my phone in my pocket buzzed. And buzzed and buzzed, like the barrage of shots we took at the end of the night. It must have just connected to the apartment Wi-Fi.

I took out my phone and saw notifications on the screen: my parents had called literally dozens of times since I had left for the bar. Not through my number, because that was deactivated internationally, but on Skype. FaceTime. Facebook Messenger. I didn't even know you could call people on Facebook Messenger.

Drunk as hell, I called them back like it was a reflex. "Mom and Dad?" I said, as if it was a normal phone call.

"Amir! Where are you?" My mom was having a heart attack through the phone. "We've been worried sick," she said, her voice sharp as knives. "And whatever is going on, we need you to talk to us."

I sobered up immediately. "I can't," I said. But I could only act so sober. "I can't." I choked. "I can't. I can't. I can't . . ."

"You're scaring us," my dad said. I could picture him through the line, holding my mom. "First you skip your graduation ceremony, and now you're scaring us. Is it college? You worked so hard in high school, and we didn't mean to put pressure on you with those rejections."

The knot in my stomach grew so tight. "It's not that," I said. That knot had stitched my mouth shut. Even though I had distance, even though I was safe, I still couldn't say the words.

I bit my lip, hard. The points just didn't add up.

My family was still on the phone. "Amir, is it the pressure?" my dad said. "We thought you'd come home, like the last time you . . . went off like this. But we don't even know where you are. Please, you can talk to us."

Could I, though?

Something shifted in me, right there, and I stayed quiet.

In a lot of ways, I'm lucky. I know that. I get to exist at a time when being different is okay. My generation *embraces* its differences. But sometimes, when I feel like my family doesn't understand, *can't* understand, who I am . . . I wish I were different in a different way.

"Amir . . . *joonam, azizum* . . ."

The tally system is only necessary when you're different from your family. Being Iranian and Muslim is one thing—it comes with its own set of challenges—but at least my mom, dad, Soraya, and I fight those battles together. We deal with the same shitty remarks, the same stares, the same stereotypes. But when you're gay—your family isn't different like you anymore. They don't understand. And worst of all, they might hate you for it. The family you were born into, the people who are supposed to love you no matter what, might hate you.

"Amir," my mom snapped. She was growing frustrated. "Enough is enough. This is all very American of you. This whole running away thing is American. Come *home*."

That's what my parents said about gay people, the one time the topic came up at the dinner table: "It's an American thing. It's part of their culture. Not ours." I remember sitting there quietly as Soraya argued with them, my heart sinking in my chest.

Sometimes I would tell myself that if I'd just been born into a nice, liberal, *American* family, none of this would be a problem. I wouldn't be a double whammy. I would just be me.

The line got silent. "I have to go," I said, ending the call.

Interrogation Room 38

Roya Azadi

I WAS TERRIFIED *after that phone call. If I could have just known what was on Amir's mind—if I could tell him he could trust me, that we could just talk about it . . . In any case, I remember I looked at my husband differently after Amir hung up. Before, he had assured me that Amir would come home, that it was just like the last time he had left home. Something had happened, and he needed to get away for a few days. But this wasn't like the last time anymore. Or maybe it was. Because the last time Amir had run away, it had been over a comment. My husband had said—he had said something unkind about a trans . . . transgender woman on television, and he and Amir got into an argument. Amir called us backward, and he stormed out of the house and didn't come home until the next day.*

We did not call the police then. And we certainly couldn't call them this time. Our son was eighteen. We knew well enough that they couldn't make an eighteen-year-old come home. And we didn't want it to look bad for Amir, that he had left home.

We told Soraya we were in touch with Amir. She asked to talk to him herself, but we said he needed space. That we were handling it.

I keep thinking back to the last time. The last time, Amir came home on his own. The last time, he didn't pick up when we called him. The last time, he just walked back into the house the next day, saying salaam, *as if he had just come home from the grocery store, and before my husband could raise his voice, I clenched his hand and said* salaam *back to our son. We never talked about it. It was as if Amir had never left.*

Now I see the bigger picture.

Twenty-Eight Days Ago

I HAD TO check out of my Airbnb that day. Waking up was a struggle, not just because of the anvils pounding against my head, but because I had the fuzziest memory of that phone call with my parents. I knew this much: it did not go well, and they still didn't know, and I would not be going home.

After I packed up, I stood outside on Via Della Gensola, the little street with the clay windowsills, the motorcycles parked along the walls, the whispers of Italian conversation flowing out the windows. What was my next move?

I managed to bum around Rome for a few hours. In a café. On some steps. And then I remembered: Jahan lived nearby. I thought I'd go ask him for advice—whether I should stay in Rome, what I should say to my parents. He seemed to know everything, and he'd been in my boat before, or at least half of it, with his Iranian dad.

Jahan's apartment was across the street from an art gallery–themed café in Trastevere, I remembered—"I like to look at the artwork from my window," he had mentioned the night before. I didn't know which unit was his, so I buzzed every single one. I got a few angry and confused Italians, but eventually I got Jahan. He let me up.

When he opened the door, Jahan was buttoning up a short-sleeved shirt with dinosaurs printed all over. "What a surprise. It's the American!" he exclaimed. "I'm getting dressed for a dinner party at my friend Giovanni's. Would you like to join?"

"Oh no," I said, flustered. "I wouldn't want to intrude."

"Don't *taarof* me, Amir. I invited you. Accept."

I couldn't help but smile. *Taarof*—the Iranian tradition of pretending to turn something down out of politeness. And hey, it's not every day you're invited to an Italian dinner party. I'd figure out a place to stay later. I accepted Jahan's invitation, he told me to leave my duffel in a corner next to a stack of poetry books—he didn't ask any questions—and we took off.

The apartment was gigantic. It took up three floors in an old building in Monti, a neighborhood near the Colosseum. It was like entering a museum, with marble busts and antiques sprinkled around, and a twelve-foot-tall painting hanging over the dining room table. The apartment belonged to Giovanni Marcello di Napoli, who opened the door and air-kissed Jahan on each cheek. Giovanni was wearing a tight black shirt, tight jeans, and a belt with the letter G on it. I guess he really liked his name. He led us through an ornate room to a group of men, all fit, all wearing tank tops or tight T-shirts.

Dinner wouldn't be served for another hour, so we floated

around the room. Everyone was in their late twenties, like Jahan, maybe their early thirties. Jahan introduced me to his friends, and I felt like I stood out like a sore thumb. It wasn't just the age difference. One of them was wearing hoop earrings. Another had pristinely arched eyebrows and spoke with a strong lisp. I thought being around people like me would feel like the perfect shoe fit, but instead, it felt like I had stepped into high heels.

-15: Might not get along with other gay men.

"Ciao, Giovanni!" I heard from the other room. I recognized the voice, even though I'd only heard it speaking English before. It was like an avalanche, the way that perfect human rushed right back into my mind. The mess of brown hair. The perfectly symmetrical face. The not-too-muscular arms and tousle of chest hair poking out of his loose tank top.

I was standing next to the big painting—a Caravaggio, Jahan had told me—when Neil entered the room, and as he approached, I puffed my shoulders and bumped into the gilded frame. "I remember you!" he said, pointing at me. I swear I died right there. It's possible I literally melted into the canvas. "You're the boy from the bookstore," Neil added, and this time, I managed a smile.

We were huddled in the back of the dining room, away from everyone else. Jahan, Neil, Giovanni, me, and this naked painted lady with her arm in the air, all *ta-da* in the painting. "So, Jahan tells me you are a writer," Giovanni said, eyeing Jahan and Neil. His voice was a mix of Italian and high-society British, and if I had to describe his aesthetic, it's tank-top-monocle-chic. "Do you write books?"

"No, no," Jahan said. "He's far too young to be a novelist."

"We did meet in a bookshop," Neil added kindly.

"Who do you write for?" Giovanni asked quickly. The three of them exchanged glances, like they had already discussed my prolific writing career on some text thread. Even Caravaggio's naked lady looked suspicious.

I was about to reply when Jahan cut me off. "We know who you really are, Amir."

I froze. And then Jahan looked at the other guys, clapped his hands up to his chest and giggled. "Oh! That was far more dramatic than I intended it to be. I just meant to say, we know you're not really a writer."

"What?" I replied.

Jahan gave me a side-eye. "Oh, come on. You're hiding something. I mean, you're eighteen years old and you're in Rome, by yourself, to 'write.' Come on. Either you're the Nigerian prince of 'writers,' or some *Talented Mr. Ripley* wannabe, or something is up. You're not fooling anyone. Now, just tell us. We're your friends. What really brought you to Rome?"

I looked around frantically at the antique busts and miniature ships all over the room. It was seriously a wonder that this place didn't have air-conditioning. My armpits were damp, and my palms were slick. I was burning up. I felt exposed, I wanted no part in this conversation, and I wanted to leave. But I also wanted to know who this "talented" Mr. Ripley was, and was it a compliment? Yet another reference I didn't understand. Yay.

But then one magic line struck me like paint hitting a canvas:

we're your friends. Jahan had stated it as plain, unambiguous fact. Was that how it worked in gay world? Was being attracted to men somehow all it took to be friends—a common experience to bond us instantly and forever? In this moment, it seemed that way. It seemed these people had accepted me into their tribe for no other reason than that. And if that was the case, then it was entirely possible that they would understand why I'd lied to them. Jahan, Neil, Giovanni—they would uniquely understand why I came to Rome.

I decided I would tell them the truth.

"I was supposed to graduate high school this week," I told them. "But I ended up leaving home instead, because . . ." They formed a circle around me, leaning in closer like I was telling them a secret. "Because . . ." I got nervous. My mind raced through all the shit I'd have to explain: Jackson. The blackmail. My parents. I would have to explain the tallies, the signs, the culture. And suddenly, I wondered if these seasoned gay men maybe *wouldn't* understand my situation—if they would judge me for not having the courage to just say the words. To come out to my parents like they had.

So I switched gears: "My parents kicked me out for being gay."

Interrogation Room 37

Amir

I CAN'T HELP *but notice that you keep staring at the cut on my face. It's fresh, from yesterday morning, after my family found me in the mountains with Neil. There was a bit of a scuffle, as you've probably guessed. And it did get a little violent. But I'll get to that later.*

That was the last time I saw Neil. Yesterday. I saw Jahan three days ago. I saw Giovanni seven days ago.

Here's the thing: I could have told them the truth. I could have told them the real reason I was in Rome when they were huddled around me, just like I've been telling it to you. But to tell them the truth would have been to admit to myself that I had abandoned my family. That I wasn't brave, but a coward. No matter how many times I told myself that it wasn't my fault, that Jake had hijacked my coming out, that the numbers just didn't add up for my parents—I still felt like a terrible son.

And that's why I'm ashamed, sir. More than you could know. But right now, I'm mostly ashamed about how everything blew up in the end.

Interrogation Room 38

Soraya

SOMETHING FROM THE *vending machine? That's very nice of you, ma'am—I mean, Officer. I was getting a little hungry. What are my options? I'll definitely have the ice cream, yes. A chocolate éclair or ice cream sandwich, if you have either of those. Please don't listen to my mother; I definitely want ice cream. Thank you. This is very yummy.*

Actually, this reminds me of last summer—our last summer in Bethesda—of a time when Amir really pissed me off. There was an ice cream truck, one of those big white vans with pictures of all the different ice creams on the side, that would come into our neighborhood every morning in the summer. We knew it was coming because you could hear its loud jingle from inside the house, and the entire neighborhood would come running out. Amir and I had been going since we were kids. I was always surprised he never found it silly or juvenile as he got older, but I wasn't going to complain.

So this one time, near the end of the summer, the ice cream truck drove off without giving me my change. I had paid five dollars and needed three twenty-five back. I told Amir to go chasing after it—he was a much faster runner than I was, and I had hurt my ankle in the pool that summer—but he didn't. He said, "Don't worry. It's not worth it. I'll just give you the money." But then one of the neighborhood kids, Junior, went after it instead. He sprinted and banged on the white van, and the driver stopped and gave him my change. I was so angry at Amir. I didn't get it. Usually I liked that he wasn't like Junior; Junior was always beating people up or talking about beating people up. Boys can be really dumb about proving their manhood. But in this moment, I just wanted my brother to stand up for me and fight. And he just wasn't willing to fight.

Amir doesn't like conflict. I've always been the fighter in the family; I think that's why my parents always liked Amir better. Don't make that face, Mom, he has always been your favorite. He was the polite, well-behaved child. I was the stubborn one. But that's also why I was so determined to find him.

You probably know a thing or two about investigations. Your job is to take clues and find answers, isn't it? That was the job I assigned to myself after Amir went missing, and so before I could go off and interview the people who knew him, I had to hunt for clues in our own home. That meant looking around his room.

Amir had cleaned his room before he left. Made his bed. There wasn't a single dirty sock in his hamper. It was like the whole time he lived with us, he had been a houseguest and not my annoying older brother who kept his boxers in four different piles, one for each corner of his bed. My parents and I messed it up a little bit that first day when we went searching through his room . . . but no one had touched it since.

I went back in one afternoon when my dad was at work and my mom had run to Costco. Yes, Mom, you still went to Costco while Amir was missing. Come on, that doesn't make you look like a bad mother. Life still had to go on. You still had to buy basmati rice in bulk.

Anyway, I was pretty much a detective that whole afternoon. I slipped into Amir's room, careful not to leave a trace, and poked around.

I checked around his desk, under his bed. I went through his drawers full of college junk mail and chargers. I saved everything that might have been a clue. I found a movie stub for Jumanji, which was weird because Amir and I saw that the weekend it came out, and this ticket was for a different date. Plus, it was for a movie theater in another town.

I went and got a step stool so I could look around the shelf inside his closet. There were a ton of textbooks and notebooks up there. I went through each one of them. On the inside cover of one of his notebooks, Amir had written all these to-do list items, stuff like "haircut" and "wiki citations" that didn't seem helpful, but also stuff like "cap and gown," which meant he wasn't planning to skip graduation, right? Then I noticed a phone number scribbled in the bottom-left corner of the page.

I called the number. It rang a few times before an automated voice answered.

"We're glad you called Trevor Lifeline. If this is an emergency—"

Then it rang again, and someone picked up.

"Trevor Lifeline, this is Clark. How are you doing?" I was confused, so I didn't say anything. "Hello, are you still there?" This Clark person sounded worried now. "I understand it can be scary to make this call, and I think you're very brave—"

I hung up the phone. I'd never heard of Trevor Lifeline, but I already knew it was for people who were thinking about taking their lives.

I tried to imagine a world where my brother was gone—really gone—

and my brother's room started to feel very small and tight around me. I even had trouble breathing. Eventually, I googled Trevor Lifeline on my phone and learned that it was a suicide hotline for LGBTQ youth. When I read those words, I had to sit down on Amir's bed.

Was my brother gay?

You'll see that my mom's head is turned away right now. And for once, I'd like to defend her. Because it's not the kind of shame you're thinking of. I sort of turned my head away like that, too. It was because I was sad . . . almost disappointed. I wasn't ashamed by the possibility of my brother being gay, but by the possibility that he was hurting and I didn't even notice.

Twenty-Eight Days Ago

AFTER I FINISHED my lie, Neil placed a hand on my shoulder. He delivered a big speech about how he and his friends were my "found family" now, and as Jahan and Giovanni nodded on, my mind shifted dramatically, and all I could think was, *The hot bookseller's hand is on my shoulder. This is not a drill. There is a literal Hemsworth brother right in front of me, and his strong hand is clenching my shoulder in a gesture of sympathy.*

The actual content of Neil's kind words noodled through my brain like soggy spaghetti. I do remember I was supremely uncomfortable. It wasn't just his hand; it was the unquestionable Italian energy in the room, the fact that I had just lied to my new friends, the guilt simmering beneath the lie, the guilt for how quickly my hormones had one-upped the other guilt . . . it was all so overwhelming. An alarm was going off inside of me, and I needed to get away. I needed to catch my breath. So I stepped out of the circle. I was going to get a glass of water. Or wine. Who knows, maybe I was going to get out. But with my clammy hands balled up and my eyes glued to the floor, I collided right into one of Giovanni's friends, who was transporting meatballs. A massive. Plate. Of meatballs.

Meatballs went flying everywhere. It was like Vesuvius had erupted.

"*Cazzo!*" Giovanni's friend yelled angrily.

"*Eccolo,*" Jahan bellowed.

I sent red lava and hot magma exploding all over with my brilliantly klutzy act. Thankfully, none of it touched the art—it just splattered over my shirt and his—but still. I was mortified.

A crowd formed around me as I sputtered my apologies. Giovanni refused to let me apologize and instead led me to his bedroom—massive, by the way, just totally insane—where I took a quick shower and changed into one of his shirts. It was a blue button-down, made from the smoothest Italian thread. He watched closely as I changed into the shirt. I asked if he had something less expensive, that felt less like clouds and more like cotton, and he just clucked his tongue. "Keep it," he said. "The clouds are yours."

Obviously, we didn't have meatballs for dinner, but we had everything else. I piled pesto pistachio pasta on my plate, juicy slabs of tomato and mozzarella, and a butter chicken that was decidedly not Italian but tasted better than any other chicken that I'd ever had . . . probably because I was having it in Italy. Some people took their plates to the fancy couches in Giovanni's living room. I pulled up a chair at the desk in the office room, where Jahan and Neil were sitting. It seemed safer for me to eat next to an iMac than on an antique sofa.

Water didn't seem to be an option at this party, so I poured my-self a glass of red wine. It was dry, not sweet like I was expecting, but it went down smoothly enough.

After dinner, we reentered the living room, where Giovanni was holding court with the other boys. His face perked up when he saw me. "Gentlemen," he said, and it was like a podium had sprung underneath him. "Have you met our new friend Amir?" The others all exchanged silent smirks.

"We've all met," I told Giovanni.

"Ah, but they must meet you again. Amir is a writer. He is re-writing his life. That accident with the meatballs was merely a plot twist."

Giovanni took me under his wing. I had the distinct feeling that he just felt bad for me and had already told the other boys about how I'd ended up in Rome. I was under the impression that Giovanni was trying hard to make up for my difficult past by show-ing me just how good I had it, being at that party.

They were fascinating people, though, I have to admit. I met doctors and painters; a singer with a shaved head who had just won a minor talent competition in Italy; a Greek man with a very loud laugh; and Giovanni's boyfriend, Rocco, a macaroni artist. I'm not kidding. He makes actual art out of actual macaroni pieces.

All of a sudden, I was happy to be there. I felt lucky. The com-mon denominator in the room wasn't that everyone was gay, or that they were Italian, or that they were friends with Giovanni. It was that they were a fun, interesting group of people.

+15: Gets along with other gay men.

Most of all, the common denominator was Jahan. If these boys were a rainbow, then Jahan was their sun, the source of their light and the center of their universe. I watched the way he swept through the crowd with such wonder. He commanded the room; he always held the power, whether it was in animated conversation or in the slightest movement, the way he took a step or reached for a plate. He never second-guessed himself.

Jahan used his power to start playing music videos on YouTube, on the iMac in front of the Caravaggio and next to a bust of Julius Caesar. The party transitioned from dinner and conversation to high-energy dance party.

It was a warm evening, made even warmer by the fact that we were inside an old apartment with no air-conditioning, jumping up and down.

Jahan and the other boys took turns pulling up grainy eighties music video after music video. Some Italian, some English, but all completely unrecognizable to me.

"Who's that one?" I asked when a woman with a seriously bad spray tan in a shiny silver leotard came on-screen.

"That's *Mina!*" Neil shouted at me, sufficiently drunk by now. He got close to my face, and even with his breath smelling like alcohol, I was more than a little turned on. "She's one of the most important divas in Italian pop culture. She was like Ariana Grande in the sixties and seventies."

"That's an insult to Mina," Jahan said.

"That is an insult to Ariana Grande," one of the other boys snapped back.

It went like that for a few hours—a different diva or queer icon would come on, I'd ask who she was, and a different boy would yell at me for not recognizing her before educating me. *"Child!" "Child!" "Not again!" "SOMEONE NEEDS TO REVOKE HIS GAY CARD!"* I didn't think it was fair; these people grew up in Italy, or in Neil's case, the Castro in San Francisco, where they were surrounded by plenty of divas. I was sorely undereducated in the diva department.

These boys made it their mission to educate me.

Neil, Jahan, and I stepped outside when "Let's Have a Kiki" by the Scissor Sisters started blaring through the speakers.

"Amir, do you even know this song?" Jahan asked.

"'Let's Have a Kiki,' by the Scissor Sisters," I said.

Jahan raised his chin. "Very impressive."

"It was on the computer screen . . ." I admitted. Neil and Jahan looked at each other, rolled their eyes, and laughed.

It was raining lightly, and the three of us huddled underneath the entrance of Giovanni's apartment building. Neil propped an elbow against the arched wooden door. He ran his hand through his perfectly sweaty, greasy hair. The overhead light illuminated him like in a museum exhibit. He was pretty much the statue of David in that moment.

Jahan took out a lighter and flicked it no fewer than a dozen times before it caught fire. He lit his cigarette and looked at me appraisingly. "You're going to need more lessons if you're actually staying here," Jahan said.

That should have scared me more than it did—the idea of

permanence, of a new life in Rome—but I was drunk. I just giggled. "I think maybe I should learn Italian first," I said, "before I become an expert on divas."

Jahan scoffed. "Nonsense," he said. Then he peered at Neil. "But if you're serious about learning Italian, Neil could help you. He's a tutor, you know."

Neil and I started to object. "I'm sure Amir would prefer an actual Italian to tutor him in Italian . . ."

"Yeah, no. I mean, it's not that, I just—"

"I'll ask Francesco if he has any friends who can tutor him," Neil said. "Maybe we can even find him a hunky Italian tutor."

"Francesco?"

"His *amore*," Jahan said.

"My partner," Neil clarified. "'*Amore*' means 'love.'"

"*Amore*," I said, turning over the word, attaching it to Neil and his *partner*. I remembered what Jahan had told me last night, that Francesco was planning to propose to Neil on his birthday. "*Amore*," I repeated, giggling this time.

"Look, you're already teaching him Italian!" Jahan squealed. "So it's settled. Neil will teach you Italian and I'll teach you divas. And thus begins your education at *l'università degli omosessuali italiani*."

I couldn't even look at Neil. The prospect of studying Italian with someone that attractive just seemed too much. I wouldn't learn a thing; I would spend entire lessons trying not to stare at his face. If Jahan was the sun, then Neil was a solar eclipse; I was afraid if I looked directly at him, I might go blind.

Neil, however, just shrugged. "Hey, Jahan, how about you enroll at this university, too, instead of leaving us for the States?"

"You're going to America?" I asked.

Jahan rolled his eyes and went, "In a month, so they say."

"Like, to visit?" I asked.

"No, for good," Neil said, frowning.

I frowned, too; I was immediately filled with dread. I felt sad. More than that, I was confused with myself, with how I was capable of feeling loss before I had actually lost the thing itself. I'd felt this way before, when things ended abruptly with Jackson.

Jahan must have noticed, because he went, "Oh, don't look so dreary, Amir. Odds are looking slim right now. It depends entirely if I can pass online algebra. I never graduated from college, yet somehow they accepted me into a poetry MFA, and *somehow* that means I need to take baby math to enroll. It doesn't make any sense."

We stepped back into the apartment, and I eased into the party. I remember it had felt so aggressive at first: aggressive with the tank tops and muscled biceps, aggressive when I collided into the meatball tray and made a mess. At what point did I just let myself breathe? I think it was before the YouTube dance party, when Giovanni was parading me around. One of the Italian boys taught me this phrase, *"Che cazzo dici?"* which basically translates to "What the fuck are you saying?" That was when I accepted the absurdity of my situation, the WTF of it all, of being around all these older gay men, and eased right in. I think that's when the party stopped feeling aggressive.

Giovanni jumped up on a creaky old armchair and announced that we were moving to a bar in Testaccio, another neighborhood in Rome. It was nearly three in the morning; I couldn't believe these people still had the energy to go out. But Giovanni rallied the troops and we left the apartment, wandering the streets of Rome to our next destination.

It was a long walk—we crossed the bridge over to Trastevere, and our group was so loud and so obnoxious that half the people we passed avoided us like the plague, while the other half high-fived us and took part in our debauchery. The streets of Trastevere were cramped and alive as ever, but we marched right past every bar, every temptation. Eventually, we reached a second bridge to Testaccio. On this bridge, a group of Italian boys—they looked like teenagers, maybe even younger than me—noticed us and yelled some words at Jahan in drunken Italian before exploding into cruel laughter. I didn't need to understand what they were saying to know what had just happened. I was shocked. But Jahan just smiled. He waved the pearls he had put on at Giovanni's. And when he caught the look of shock on my face, he said: "The thing about bigots is they always go out of their way to acknowledge my fabulous existence, when I hardly notice theirs."

You see? Jahan always had the power.

Me? I'd felt powerless my whole life. This was new to me. Confidence. Power. Whatever you want to call it. But instead of feeling inspired by Jahan's words, by knowing I could be like that someday, too, I felt an itch under my shirt.

Jake's blackmail came rushing back—*You wouldn't want us to smear your faggy little secret across town, would you?* I was quiet the rest of the walk through Testaccio as the anxiety festered under my skin; I felt it through my shirt like a burning rash, and I thought that if the other boys so much as looked at me, they would see it. Could Jahan tell that I was hiding this big secret? That I was stalling a big decision? Could he tell that I wasn't totally comfortable, that I was spiraling inside my head, that I was neither here nor there?

Maybe all they could tell was that I'd had four glasses of red wine. I was drunk. Being drunk can be a great thing and a terrible thing. It can help cover up your emotions, or it can expose the hell out of them. It can help you make friends and lose them.

We arrived at Rigatteria, the bar Neil's partner had just opened. I had kind of assumed it would be a gay bar, but where he took us was the literal opposite of a gay bar. It was an antique shop. There were at least fifteen odd lamps. A wooden panel. Mismatched couches and armchairs. And it was just as empty and quiet as an antique shop. Neil explained to me that in Italian, *"rigatteria"* meant "junk shop."

But then we hit the rooftop. It was a completely different vibe upstairs, kind of like the difference between your brain before coffee and after coffee. Downstairs was decaf; the rooftop was triple espresso madness. Pretty Italian girls and handsome boys with tight jaws and even tighter shirts were dancing, and we danced alongside them. There were yellow lights, orange lights, so many lights. It was like we were at the center of the universe. If Rigatteria was a junk shop, the rooftop was its hidden treasure.

At four in the morning, Jahan did a split on the dance floor and ripped his pants. The party was as alive as ever.

At four thirty, Neil and his partner kissed. I'll admit, it made me jealous. When they came over so Neil could introduce me to Francesco, my whole body tensed and my mouth turned dry. It was a short introduction, since Francesco didn't actually speak any English, and Neil laughed and said, "Maybe I really *should* try and teach you Italian." He slapped me playfully on the back. I think Francesco noticed my cheeks turning red.

I looked around the glowing rooftop and wondered when this would all come to an end. My Italy escapade, yes. But mostly this party. I wasn't used to being out so late. Come to think of it, I wasn't used to being out, period.

At five in the morning, people were still going strong, but our group left. We headed over to Garbo, the bar where I had met Jahan, for a "nightcap"—which I learned was not an article of clothing but an alcoholic drink you have before bed. (The vocabulary around drinking is truly astonishing.) Neil stayed behind to help his boyfriend—sorry, partner—he said he preferred that term, since it felt more serious, more *committed*—clean up. At Garbo, people sat around a clump of small round tables, drinking their nightcaps and telling wild stories.

Jahan appeared from the bar with a bottle of champagne.

"It's time for a toast," he said. "To many things. Neil and Francesco's new bar. And our new friend, Amir."

He held the champagne bottle under his arm and yanked the wooden cork off, and with that decisive *pop*, I decided that I was in awe of these people. As Jahan filled the champagne glasses with bubbly, golden delight, I felt incredibly lucky. I could have been alone. I could have been home dealing with the worst kind of coming out. Instead, I was with these men, this secret society of Italians and Americans who were free to be themselves. I felt happier than I'd felt in a very long time.

Most everyone soaked up Jahan's toast, this moment, except for Rocco, Giovanni's boyfriend. He refused to sit down. He went around the bar, arbitrarily pinching strangers' nipples. (To be clear, this is *still* not the nipple story.) His boyfriend looked annoyed, but he tried his best not to intervene. He and Jahan were having a conversation. Rocco also showed off his macaroni art to me on his phone, which I pretended to be impressed with. It didn't look much more advanced than Lego pieces.

We left the bar at six in the morning. Giovanni called a taxi and went home. Rocco kept walking with Jahan and me even though I'd assumed he would go back with his boyfriend.

As we were crossing the Viale over to the other side of Trastevere, Rocco put an arm around my waist.

"Um . . ." My body turned stiff. The only other boy who had touched me like this before was Jackson.

"What do you want?" Rocco asked.

"Sleep, I think?"

"Are you sure about that . . ." he slurred.

I wasn't sure about anything. I thought Rocco was with Giovanni? He kept his hand on my waist as we kept walking; it made me uncomfortable, but I didn't want to just assume that he was hitting on me. I'd already learned that Italians kissed on both cheeks when they said hello; maybe this was their good night.

When we reached Jahan's place, Jahan cleared his throat and asked what I was doing, looking at me like *don't do that*, and I realized, as Rocco pulled me in closer, that he actually thought we were going to hook up.

I broke free from Rocco's insistent grip. "I'm staying with you, Jahan! If that's all right," I said. Jahan smiled in a relieved way. We said good night to Rocco, who didn't seem very happy with this particular outcome.

"I'm sorry about that," Jahan said as we walked up the steep, uneven stairs in his building. "Rocco can be a little . . ."

"Aggressive?"

"Drunk."

"Yeah. Not cool."

Jahan quietly fidgeted with his apartment door until it opened.

As we were brushing our teeth next to each other in the bathroom, Jahan smiled at me in the mirror. "I hope my friends didn't *completely* scare you off tonight," he said. Some toothpaste dribbled down the side of his cheek.

"Are you kidding?" I said. "I had the best time."

"Of course you did. It was practically a Fellini film tonight. You know, I've been trying to convince all those guys to re-create the orgy scene from *La Dolce Vita* for years now—some would prefer to call it a party, but, I mean, it's the *climax* of the movie for a reason . . ." Jahan looked at me like I was supposed to get the reference. "You're kidding me. Not even *La Dolce Vita?* Oh, Amir. We'll have to fix that. Now, I don't know what your plan is for tomorrow and the rest of your time here—"

"I don't really have a plan—"

"—but you can stay at my apartment for as long as you need."

"No, no," I said, gargling water. "I couldn't."

Jahan spit in the sink. "Didn't anyone ever tell you not to *taarof* with your mouth full, Amir *joon?*" He handed me a towel. "I insist."

"Well, that's very kind of you, but I'll get out of your hair—"

"*Nah, baba,*" he said, waving a hand dismissively. "You are more than welcome here. I would be thrilled to have you. Ecstatic. Elated!" A playful smirk crossed his face. "How's that for Persian hospitality?"

I don't know why, but every time Jahan used a Farsi word or mentioned being Persian, I did a little cartwheel inside. He didn't keep his halves separate. He was Iranian. He was gay. He was all of that in the same breath. I'd never met someone like Jahan, a double whammy like me, who embraced both sides—every side— of himself.

Interrogation Room 38

Soraya

MY FRIEND MADISON'S *brother goes to Amir's high school, and she told me her brother and his friends all hung out in the food court of the mall. So that's where I went. It took me a couple of days after I made that discovery, though, since I had morning-to-night rehearsals. We were learning the choreography to "Jellicle Songs for Jellicle Cats." I was pretty drained at the end of those days. Maybe I was still processing what I'd learned about Amir.*

Anyway, I made it to the mall eventually. The food court was sad. I don't know how else to say it. If this was where high school seniors hung out, I would prefer to just stay in middle school. The lighting was terrible, and all the tables were cluttered and plain white. It was about as basic as a Starbucks frappuccino.

The seniors were in the back. They were clustered together. I nervously talked to a few of them. Most of them didn't know Amir, until one girl looked at me kind of funny and then looked over and said I should talk to this one guy Jake.

"Did you know my brother?" I asked him. "Amir." He looked at me with beady eyes. He had annoyingly twisty hair. He looked at me like he recognized me. "You should talk to Jackson Preacher," Jake said quietly.

As I walked away, I felt like he was watching me.

Twenty-Seven Days Ago

THE TV WAS blasting at full volume when I woke up on Jahan's couch. It sounded like one of those MTV-style reality competition shows: ". . . and a grand prize of one hundred thousand *doolahs*! With extra-special guest . . ."

"*Buongiorno*, sleepyhead," Jahan said. He leapt over the couch and sat down on my knees.

"Ouch!" I yanked my feet out from underneath him. "What time is it?"

"Two in the afternoon," a voice with an Italian accent said.

"What? Ugh," I groaned. Slowly, I rubbed my eyes and looked around the living room. Someone was sitting in the armchair. A girl. Maybe Jahan's roommate? I couldn't remember if Jahan had a roommate. "*Buongiorno*," I said to her.

She and Jahan kept their eyes glued to the TV.

"What is that?" I asked. My head hurt. Miraculously, there was a glass of water on the coffee table, next to my phone.

"*RuPaul's Drag Race*," Jahan said. "It's our Sunday church."

I took a big sip of water, and it was like the pearly gates of heaven had opened in my mouth. I picked up my phone and saw that I had a text from Neil, whose WhatsApp profile picture—at some beach, leaning forward, smiling—woke me up in other ways.

> If you still want to start those tutoring lessons, I finish up
> at the bookstore at 5 today. Meet me there?

Whoa.

I also noticed I didn't have any missed calls or texts from my parents. When I first got to Rome, they were calling nonstop; now, I hadn't heard from them in almost two days. That worried me. I wondered if Jake finally decided to pull the trigger and spill my secret. If my mom and dad had already erased me from their lives.

I got up off the couch and went to the bathroom to get my shit together. My hair looked moppy as hell. When I came back into the living room, there were a bunch of drag queens lined up in a row on the TV screen.

Jahan looked at me funny. "You look like you're watching aliens descend upon earth for the first time."

"No, I—it's just . . ."

"You've never seen a drag queen before, have you?"

I shrugged. "They kind of remind me of clowns."

Jahan shook his head. He scooted over on the couch and gestured for me to sit next to him.

"Do you see that?" Jahan pointed at a drag queen who had just come out of a limo wearing a sparkly jumpsuit and a big white wig. "A clown would *never.*"

He was right. Drag queens were far more advanced than clowns. I had never watched *RuPaul's Drag Race* before, but it didn't take long before I was asking questions about the rules and the competitors. It was like *America's Next Top Model* but with men in high heels. And the shade. These people threw incredible amounts of shade.

+10: Enjoys *RuPaul's Drag Race.*

During the lip-sync portion, I texted Neil back.

> Buongiorno.

Neil responded:

> Wow, you're already fluent! Maybe you don't need me after all . . .

I wrote back immediately.

> Beginner's luck.

He replied:

> So what you're saying is you still need a tutor?

I paused.

How do you say yes in Italian?

Neil wrote:

Sí. Like Spanish. Perfetto. Meet at the bookstore then?

I started to type out "see you there," but I just sent a thumbs-up emoji.

After the *Drag Race* episode ended—a tall white queen appropriately named "Milk" got eliminated—Jahan's friend left, and Jahan went into the kitchen to make pasta. I kept checking my phone to see if my parents had decided to call or text.

"Everything okay?" Jahan asked as we were eating. I had hardly touched my food. "Fine. I'll fess up. The Bolognese sauce came from a jar. I have clearly ruined Italian food for you. You can go home now."

Home. Jahan winced at his word choice.

"Sorry," he said. "I know you can't . . ."

His voice trailed off. He was right, though. Because if Jake really did tell my family, I couldn't go back home. I imagined showing up at our doorstep, meeting my parents' blank stares. They wouldn't recognize me. They would only see the person in that photo, kissing Jackson in the car.

"Don't worry about it," I said to Jahan.

He nodded. "What'd you think of *Drag Race*?" Jahan asked.

I forced down a bite of pasta. "It was good," I said, chewing, swallowing. "You and your friend seem to really be into it."

Jahan's eyes lit up. "Oh, we're obsessed. You know why? Because drag queens don't give a shit. There is no group of people on this planet that gives less of a shit than drag queens. People can call them freaks, say they're confused or sick or whatever, and they don't give a shit about any of it."

I smiled. "Even clowns care what people think of them," I said.

"Oh, clowns are the most fragile bitches in the world. They can hardly take criticism. Trust me. I've dated enough clowns to know. Drag queens, though"—Jahan made a chef's kiss with his fingers—"ugh, I just love them."

"Also, on a technical level," I said, swallowing down another bite of pasta, "it's amazing how they can just transform like that."

"Exactly! They transform. They sing. They have fabulous wigs. They're like—what's the name of that Disney star who was a regular girl but secretly a pop star at night?"

"Hannah Montana."

"Right. I knew it was something Midwestern. Anyway, drag queens are like Hannah Montana but less tacky."

"First of all, how *dare* you diss Hannah Montana like that?" I said, pointing my fork at Jahan. "Second, I don't think Montana is even in the Midwest. It's technically part of the Northwest."

"How the hell do you know that?"

"I . . . once spent a whole Saturday editing all the Wikipedia pages for the different geographic regions in America?"

"I'm not even going to ask." Jahan ruffled my hair. "Weirdo."

"Says the guy who watches drag queens on TV every Sunday."

"Well, it sounds to me like you've come around on the matter of drag queens," Jahan said, winking at me. "You thought they were like clowns, but they're so much more. See? You just had to give them a chance."

I told Jahan I was meeting Neil soon for our first lesson.

"What are you doing today?" I asked.

"I was going to go to Naples—it's such an easy day trip from Rome—but that seems out of the question now, doesn't it?" Jahan sighed. "I should really do my algebra homework. I'm a few lessons behind."

"So you're working?"

"Probably not. It's too lovely a day to be responsible. If we're being honest, I think I'll just head down to that café across the street and, oh, I don't know." He gestured out the window. "Maybe write."

"A poem?"

Jahan shrugged. "Possibly. Or something else might catch my attention. A friend. An aperitivo. I can't control these things."

The bookstore was still busy when I arrived. Neil asked me to hang tight for a minute while he moved around the store, recommended books, plucked them off the shelves. He was friendly to everyone he interacted with, even as he wiped beads of sweat off his forehead. His Big Bookseller Energy was on full display.

"All right," Neil said after the door jingled behind the last customer. He grabbed his shoulder bag from behind the checkout desk. "Let's go."

We made our way to Rigatteria, where there would be more space to spread out and have our lesson. Even walking next to him, I couldn't bear to look at Neil. It was like God had neatly hidden a secret Ryan Reynolds lookalike in Italy, far away from the tabloids but right before my very hormonal eyes.

"Are you okay?" he asked. "You're being awfully quiet."

"Sorry," I said. "I'm just tired from last night."

"You're telling me. I got maybe two hours of sleep," Neil said.

I tried looking at Neil, but my eyes just leapt over him to the Tiber River. We were crossing the same same bridge over the Tiber River as the night before, the one where those Italian boys heckled us. "I appreciate you doing this," I said.

"Oh! I wasn't trying to make you feel bad," he said. "Trust me, I'm happy to be sleep deprived. We haven't had a night like that in a long time."

"Really? I assumed you guys did that all the time." I kept my eyes focused on the shimmering water. A bunch of food stands and white tents were setting up along the edge of the river.

Neil laughed. "We used to, but then everyone grew up. Became boring. Got boyfriends. I know Francesco and I look like we're thirty, but trust me, we're seventy on the inside. Don't ever get a boyfriend, Amir."

I rolled my eyes. "What, are you my dad now?"

"Maybe your daddy . . ."

Oh my God.

"Just kidding," Neil said. "You probably don't even know what that means."

"Hey, just because I came out like five seconds ago doesn't mean I don't know what a daddy is!" I defended. "I've been on the internet. I know who Anderson Cooper is."

Neil shook his head. Now that we were joking around, I was able to look at him. It was just like when I had cheated in that first un-staring contest with Jackson, when I snuck that first glance.

"Anyway," Neil continued, "I think this summer will be different, actually. You know Jahan is leaving in a few weeks, that bastard. We're all devastated. But I can already tell that our friends are more willing to come out, see him, do things, now that it's our last summer together. Plus, we have Rigatteria. Italians love their rooftops when it's warm out. You're catching us at a good time."

For a moment, I closed my eyes and let myself imagine an entire summer with these people. I drew the picture in my head, and it was a masterpiece.

We arrived at Rigatteria. Neil had a fresh notebook for me, which I felt stupid for not bringing myself. We said *"ciao"* to Francesco, who was cleaning the rooftop, and found a small cherry desk by the downstairs bar. It was old and lit only by the dim glow of a green desk lamp. Neil started the lesson by teaching me the alphabet and numbers, and eventually we moved on to some basic vocabulary.

"*'Avere'* is the verb for 'to have,'" Neil said. He wrote it down in my notebook. "But it's an irregular conjugation. *'Io ho,'* I have. *'Tu hai,'* you have. *Lei, lui, lei ha . . ."*

When Neil would reach over to write down a word, his forearm kept brushing my wrist. It meant nothing to him but stirred everything in me. My skin became electric. It wasn't just the touch. It was the setup, too. Francesco eventually made his way downstairs to clean up the area behind us. I felt like he was watching us, could sense that every fiber of my being was aroused as Neil spoke softly and filled my notebook with Italian words.

It was a good thing Neil was writing everything down. I would have to review it all later, when I was less distracted.

Toward the end of our lesson, I asked Neil, "What's the word for 'question' in Italian?"

"Domanda," he said.

"All right. I have a *domanda. Io. Ho. Domanda,"* I said, making sure to use the right verb conjugation. "What's the deal with Rocco?"

Neil reached for my notebook and wrote: *Io ho una domanda.* Damn. I was close. "I actually don't know Rocco very well. He and Jahan used to work together in a pizza shop, I think, or some kind of tourist trap in Piazza Navona, way before we were all friends. That's how they got close. When I first met Rocco, I just knew him as Jahan's artsy friend."

"But he's with Giovanni, right?" I asked.

Neil's eyes shifted. "Yes."

I sat in silence for a few seconds. Neil asked why I was asking about Rocco, and I explained to him what happened last night.

"Oh boy," he said, though he didn't seem surprised. "I'm sorry."

"What I don't get," I said, "is why Rocco would hit on me if he's dating Giovanni."

"Well. Yeah," Neil said. "But they're open." I cocked my head back. "It means they're not monogamous. They're allowed to hook up with other people."

"I know what an open relationship is," I said defensively.

"Right, because you're on the 'internet,'" Neil mocked.

I glared at Neil, but he was right; I knew what it meant abstractly, the way you know a billionaire is a person with billions of dollars, but to see it applied in the flesh, to real-life people I had met, was new to me.

"So, um. Is that . . . common?" I asked.

Neil laughed. "I don't know. A lot of gay couples are open. I have some straight friends who are in open relationships, too."

"But isn't the point of a relationship that you're with one person?"

"Depends on your definition of a relationship. Some people would insist that a relationship is only between a man and a woman."

"Good point," I said. "I guess if you look at it like that, anything works."

"Yeah. Though I don't want you thinking every gay couple is open." He lowered his voice and looked over his shoulder. "Francesco and I aren't open." The way he said it, almost emphasizing it, I felt like he was making a point. "There's nothing wrong with it, but it's not for everyone. It just comes down to what you're most comfortable with."

Suddenly, I felt guilty about my feelings or hormones or whatever I was experiencing around Neil. I shouldn't have been lusting after someone who not only had a boyfriend, but was kind enough to tutor me in Italian. Things like this don't work out when they're secret or forbidden. Exhibit A: Jackson.

Neil ended our lesson with some helpful phrases like *"come si dice"* (how do you say . . .) and *"vorrei"* (I would like . . .), phrases I could use to get around Rome, and he asked if this time next Sunday worked for our next lesson. I realized he had assumed that I was really staying in Italy. I needed to figure that out.

I hesitated. "Um, sure." It also occurred to me we had never discussed payment, which seemed especially stupid on my part considering I was on a limited budget. "How much do I owe you for the lesson?"

"No, no. Please," Neil scoffed. "I'm not charging you."

"What? Come on. Please." I started to pull euros out of my front pocket, but Neil shoved my hand back.

"You're a friend," Neil insisted. He held my wrist and looked me straight in the eyes. I nearly had a heart attack. "Don't worry about it."

I smiled. "Thanks."

Neil walked me to the door and gave me directions for getting back to Trastevere, even though I told him I had Jahan's address saved on my phone. I thanked him one more time for the lesson and said *"arrivederci."* Neil corrected me.

"*'Arrivederci'* is more formal. You should use *'ciao,'* or *'a dopo.'*"

"What does *'a dopo'* mean?"

"See you later," Neil said. "Or *'a presto.'* That means 'see you soon.'"

I considered my options. *"A presto."*

"A presto."

Interrogation Room 38

Soraya

THE DAY AFTER *I talked to Jake at the mall, I met with Jackson Preacher at Starbucks. He was wearing a polo shirt and khaki shorts, with brown flip-flops. He was cracking his knuckles.*

How did I get there? Mom, don't act so surprised. You drove me. Sort of. You dropped me off at the movie theater next door. I said I was seeing the new Mamma Mia *movie with Madison. There is no new* Mamma Mia *movie. Besides, even if there were, you know Madison's mom doesn't let her watch PG-13 movies. I'm sorry I lied.*

Jackson was super friendly. He bought me a pastry. Though he seemed nervous, too. When I messaged him on Instagram the day before, he messaged back right away, like, less than a minute later. He asked if we had heard from Amir. I thought that was kind of weird. Either this guy murdered my brother or Amir actually had a friend at school.

We started talking, and it was obvious we were both being careful with our words. I didn't want to out Amir, in case Jackson didn't know, so I said things like "I feel like he's hiding something" and "I wish I could know the real Amir."

Jackson took a big sip of his coffee and went, "You know, don't you?" Again, I tiptoed. I wasn't sure if Jackson was the villain here or what. Maybe he was the reason Amir left. Maybe he had made Amir believe that our family wouldn't love him. Jackson took one more sip, then chugged the rest of his drink and said we should go for a walk.

We found a bench in a park and sat down. Jackson kept taking deep breaths, looking around, shaking his knee. I had a feeling I knew what was going on at this point, so I asked: "Jackson, were you my brother's boyfriend?" He broke down. I couldn't believe it, this football player, his hands covering his face. He told me he hadn't ever talked to anyone about this, any of this—no one knew that he was gay except for Amir. But they had stopped talking a couple of months before graduation.

I asked Jackson why they stopped talking. He said Amir just stopped texting him, made up excuses and stopped wanting to hang out. He knew something was wrong. Jackson thought maybe it was something at home, because when he asked if it had to do with his parents, Amir got really snappy. He said Amir couldn't even look at him.

The last thing I asked Jackson on that park bench was "Did you love my brother?" Jackson thought for a bit, and then he said, "I loved how he made me feel."

I asked, "How was that?"

He said, "Like myself."

Interrogation Room 37

Amir

WHAT'S MY RELATIONSHIP *with my sister like? I love her. I admire the hell out of her. I think she's the most talented person I know.*

The first time I saw my sister in a musical, she played one of the boys in Newsies, *and I'm telling you, she was electric up there. The way she tapped her feet on that stage, tipped her hat, the way her face was dirtied up but glowing the entire time—it was unforgettable. That was four summers ago. She did* The Music Man *the next summer,* Honk! *the summer after that, and then last summer, because we were moving, she wasn't able to do a musical. That's why I was so happy she got the role she wanted in* Cats *this summer.*

I felt awful leaving her. But I felt worse my last few weeks at home, because Soraya was so happy about her role and I was so miserable. I didn't want to ruin her happiness. That's why I didn't tell her I was running away. Pretty stupid, right?

She texted me right after that first phone call in the airport: WTF, Amir. *Drama always suited her. It was like a flood of texts after that:*

What's going on? Where are you? Why did you skip your graduation? You're so dumb.

I told her I would come home soon. That was a lie, but I couldn't crush Soraya. She kept begging me for an explanation, which just tightened the guilty feeling in my chest more. But I couldn't drag her down with me. I made her promise to stay focused on the musical. I told her I couldn't wait to see her in it, that I wouldn't miss it for the world.

Twenty-Four Days Ago

I HAD BEEN staring at the text on my phone for a full minute. *I know you're gay.*

It was seven thirty a.m. This couldn't be real.

I looked around at Jahan's living room. Everything looked so peaceful under the soft morning light. The couch I had woken up on. The stack of books at the foot of the couch. The pasta machine on the kitchen counter, the dishes Jahan and I had been too lazy to wash, the Joni Mitchell album he'd played for me.

All those things were real. Not this text from my sister, the words I had been dreading my entire life.

You know I don't care, right? read her next text. You know I love you.

The smell of espresso rose up through the window from the café below. Slowly, I started breathing again. I wrote back: Do mom and dad know?

I waited for a response. Finally, Soraya's WhatsApp status changed to "Online." She typed, then deleted. Then typed again.

No. Of course not. Next text: Why don't you tell them?

You know I can't tell them. I was pounding the letters on my phone's keyboard. That's a stupid question, Soraya. Come on.

You know Dad spent the last two days looking for you in New York, Soraya wrote back. He literally went looking for you there.

I took a deep breath. I felt sick to my stomach. To my dad, I was still the old Amir. I wasn't the person watching drag queens on TV with Jahan and talking about open relationships with Neil. I wasn't a stranger who had been living in his house. Not yet.

Remember the scoreboard, I thought to myself. *The numbers aren't in your favor.*

How did you find out? I asked Soraya.

I talked to Jackson. Fuck. What did Jackson tell her? Before I could ask, Soraya texted again. It doesn't matter. Come home, Amir.

I can't come home.

My sister and I usually texted with memes and emojis. We'd never texted with this many full sentences before, this many periods. It was just that kind of conversation.

If I come home, I wrote, I'll have to tell them.

Or you could make up another excuse, she texted.

That didn't sit well with me. Lying, again. I'd done it my whole life, but after these days in Rome, I just couldn't see myself pretending the reason I ran away was because I didn't feel like crossing the graduation stage or some other bullshit like that. I didn't reply. Soraya texted again: Where are you now?

As much as my home life had gone to shit, I couldn't stop thinking about the other night with Jahan and his friends, dancing on the rooftop into the early morning . . . I wanted more of that. I was hungry for more of that. Life. Authentic, unapologetic life. I wanted to sink my teeth into that kind of living, the kind I'd never thought I would have.

And Jahan. I had grown so comfortable around him. We had absolutely nothing in common, and yet we had everything in common.

I didn't know what to say to Soraya. Whatever, she finally texted. I still wish you had come out to me. I do musical theater. I've been around gay people forever. I'm honestly kind of offended you didn't think you could tell me.

I threw myself down on the couch, sighing deeply.

A few minutes later, Jahan stumbled out of his room. I watched him hobble past me in his red checkered boxers and into the kitchen.

"You're up awfully early," he said.

"So are you," I said.

"Trust me, I am nowhere *near* awake." Jahan came out of the kitchen with a glass of water. He leaned against a wall that was covered in Polaroids and took a long sip, glancing over at me on the couch. "Everything okay?"

No. My sister found out I'm gay. I haven't talked to my parents in days. I don't know what to do next.

I looked at Jahan. He could barely keep his eyes open.

"Yeah, everything is fine," I said.

Jahan nodded sleepily. "Keys are on the shelf by the door," he said. He went back into his room and closed the door.

I willed myself to leave the apartment. It was the closest thing I had to a routine these past couple of mornings while Jahan slept in until the afternoon. Much like with capitalism and heteronormativity, Jahan believed mornings to be an oppressive construct and made it his personal mission to disregard them.

It was a particularly peaceful morning in Trastevere. A lot of shops hadn't even opened yet. Even though some of the streets were starting to look familiar to me, I was still in awe of it all: the moss-covered walls, the clothes hanging out the windows, the narrow alleys that opened into wide piazzas.

A morning walk can seriously be like therapy.

I found a restaurant on Isola Tiberina, a small island on the Tiber River, and sat down at a table outside. The other tables around me were empty. I had noticed that most Italians didn't sit down to have coffee, but instead had their espresso shots standing up at the counter. They were so cool about it. They would just roll in and order *un caffè*, maybe make some small talk with the barista, and then knock back the shot of espresso and drop a euro and say *"ciao"* before hopping back on their mopeds.

After the waitress took my order, I reached into my backpack to check my money. It was all twenties and fifties. I had some single euro coins in my pocket. All in all, I had about eight hundred euros left from what I'd taken out at the airport, carefully split among my backpack, duffel, and various pockets.

Still, I was starting to worry about money. I took out my laptop and opened the Wikipedia page for this cryptocurrency start-up that had asked me to make a couple of edits to their Controversies section. It was a little sketchy, but they were offering me a thousand bucks (in real money) for *very* little work.

The waitress came out with my coffee, in a little white espresso cup on a little white saucer.

"*Grazie,*" I said.

Then she noticed my laptop on the table and frowned.

"I am sorry," she said, "but we do not allow laptops here."

"Shoot. I should have asked before I ordered," I said. "Do you know anywhere in Rome that's good for working?"

"Like Starbucks? We do not have such places here." She thought for a second. "Let me ask my manager."

The manager was a burly man with a thick head of gray hair. He introduced himself as Roberto. "I apologize," he said to me, "but we cannot have anyone working in our restaurant. I do know a café in Monti. I believe it is called Gatsby. Many students work there, on the second floor."

I looked up Gatsby Café on my phone, and it was a forty-minute walk. I sighed.

"It's all right, I'll find somewhere else."

"Are you a student?" he asked.

I shook my head.

The man looked at my computer screen. "Ah, a coder!"

I laughed. "Not exactly. I'm editing a Wikipedia page."

He scrunched his face. I explained, "Wikipedia—it's an online encyclopedia." I opened another tab that showed a finished page.

"Ahhhh, *Weekeepehdia!*" His face lit up. "You should make page for my daughter. She is very, very talented. I always tell her, *Laura, you are so talented! Rising star!* You need a page on this, this *Weekeepehdia*. She is a singer, Laura. Laura Pedrotti, look her up. Very talented." He was waving his hands in excitement. "And she is in school in America! She finished her first year at Harvard."

I googled Laura Pedrotti, and as much as I assumed the guy was just being a proud dad, she was in fact legit. She had been profiled in the *Harvard Crimson* and had one song with millions of Spotify streams; it was in a Nespresso commercial.

Then I had an idea.

"If I make your daughter a Wikipedia page," I asked Mr. Pedrotti, "could I stay and work out of your restaurant sometimes?"

He thought for a second and shrugged. "Laura Pedrotti on *Weekeepehdia. Perfetto!* Okay!"

That night, I was back at Garbo, the bar where I had met Jahan. He was hosting a literature night where anyone could get up and read something. It could be something they wrote or just something they really liked. A poem, or a scene from a novel. I wasn't really in the mood, but Jahan said if I didn't go he would kick me out of the apartment, and I didn't really feel like testing him, so I went.

The bar was buzzing with people. All sorts of characters. Men and women. An artistic crowd. These people wore funny hats, had interesting tattoos, looked at me with judgment, and I was honored—honored, I tell you—to have been judged by some of them. Women wore dark eyeliner. Men wore tight pants and loose dress shirts and held cigarettes between their fingers. Smoke swirled in the air above them.

The reading itself was a grand, sweaty affair. There was one woman with a giant tattoo over her chest that read FEMME RAGE in block letters, who read a feministy poem. I really liked it. I thought Soraya would have liked it, too. Jahan read a few quatrains—Rumi poems. The whole thing was intoxicating.

After the reading, everyone returned to drinking and smoking and socializing. Jahan went back behind the bar. He was wearing an oversized pink polo shirt. I remembered it was Wednesday, and I smiled.

"Nice *Mean Girls* reference," I said, pointing at the shirt.

He looked at me confused.

I looked at him even more confused. "Please tell me you've seen *Mean Girls*."

"That would not be an accurate statement," Jahan said.

"Jahan."

"Oh, give me a break."

"*Jahan*." I slammed my hands down on the bar. "You are literally participating in an inside joke from one of the greatest cultural phenomena of the twenty-first century, a masterpiece of American letters, and you have no idea."

I explained the joke to him. Jahan asked me which character he would be, and I told him probably Damien, who was "too gay to function."

"I take offense to that," Jahan said. "I function perfectly fine."

"That's not the point! You're missing the point!"

"Says the boy who missed the orgy scene in *La Dolce Vita*."

"First of all, I was tired and falling asleep," I said. "Second, there was no orgy! They just had a pillow fight. I might be a virgin, but I'm gonna need a little more than that if you're going to call it an 'orgy' scene."

"Is there an orgy in *Mean Girls*?"

"Um. No." I thought for a second. "But there's a scene where two of the girls transform into wild animals and fight over a hot guy?"

"Ooh, animal kingdom realness," Jahan said, making little claws with his hands.

I laughed. "Seriously, Jahan. Do you know any pop culture?" I began to quiz him while he poured drinks at the bar, and the results were abysmal. He'd never heard of Selena Gomez. He couldn't name a single Taylor Swift song.

"Not even Tay-Tay?" I said.

Jahan shook his head. "Not even . . . I'm sorry, but I refuse to acknowledge that nickname."

"I think I've figured it out," I said. "Look. I don't know pop culture before the two thousands, and you don't know pop culture after. That makes Britney Spears our cutoff."

"What is this about Britney?" Pier Paolo, one of Jahan's friends, elbowed his way to the bar. He was short and had curly black hair that bounced like springs.

"I'm a slaaaave for you." Neil came up from behind and hooked an arm around my neck.

"Pier Paolo, Neil, have you heard of Selena Gomez?" Jahan asked.

Pier Paolo shrugged.

"Isn't that the chick who dated Justin Bieber?" Neil said.

"Exactly!" I said, pointing a finger in the air. "See, I might not know Joni Mitchell and Cher—"

Neil unhooked his arm from my neck. "YOU DON'T KNOW WHO CHER IS?" he bellowed.

"I mean, I know she likes to tweet with a lot of capital letters and emojis," I said. "I just can't name any of her songs. But I know she's a big deal. You know what else is a big deal? *Mean Girls*. I've seen that movie at least fifteen times."

+15: Has seen *Mean Girls* no fewer than fifteen times. (I really shouldn't be awarded points for this, because do we get points for breathing? No. But I'm the scorekeeper.)

I noticed Jahan smiling at me out of the corner of my eye, like he enjoyed watching me take charge, school the others on *my* pop culture. He suggested we all get together at his apartment to watch the movie that night, after the bar closed.

A small group of us went back to Jahan's apartment sometime after four a.m. First, we had to find the movie online, and then Jahan had to fidget with his laptop and some kind of connecting cord, but we got it playing on the TV eventually.

After the movie ended, I asked Jahan what he thought.

"Solidly fetch," he said, nodding.

The room broke into conversation, then full-on debate. Jahan argued that Cady Heron as a protagonist followed the classic Greek hero's journey, whereas Giovanni believed it was more of a social satire that didn't adhere to strict archetypes. People referenced Shakespeare and Greek tragedies. They spoke in a mix of Italian and English. Hands were waving; fingers were pinched. I didn't realize Italians actually did that.

I sank deep into the cushion and smiled as the room grew more animated. Jahan and Pier Paolo. Neil and Giovanni. The FEMME RAGE woman. They were all so grown-up, having grown-up conversations. Outside, the sky was turning bright blue. I was drifting in and out of sleep. But they were awake and alive as ever.

Interrogation Room 38

Roya Azadi

AT THE FARSI *school where I teach, I asked one of my students who was two years below Amir at the high school if she had heard anything. She said there had been some rumors going around that semester—there was clearly something this girl didn't want to tell me. Then she said she would pray for Amir to come home. That was strange, I thought. We hadn't told anyone Amir was gone.*

I wondered: How did she find out?

Interrogation Room 38

Soraya

ONE NIGHT AFTER *rehearsal, my mom and dad were waiting for me in the kitchen. They asked me to sit down. I knew it was serious because my mom poured herself a glass of tea and didn't add any sugar cubes or have any cookies with it. She said, "I've heard some things from my students, Soraya. What have you been telling people?"*

I was kind of speechless. I thought she knew. I was all, "It shouldn't have to be private. I hate how we don't talk about these things. We just let them bottle up." My mom and dad looked at me like I had transformed into a unicorn before their eyes.

"What are you talking about?" my dad said.

I went, "I'm talking about why Amir ran away."

They looked at each other this time, like they had missed something. My mom straightened her back and said, "Do you know why he ran away, Soraya?" And my dad went, "If you know something, you need to tell us."

I was stuck. I realized my parents might not actually know. Or if they did know, they were testing me.

Word was going to get back to them eventually, through one of mom's nosy students or someone else at Amir's school. If this Jake person had found out about Amir and Jackson, then other people probably knew, too. It was only a matter of time. It was either going to be a stranger or me. Amir was never going to tell them.

So I did.

Interrogation Room 37

Amir

SORAYA TEXTED ME *right after she told my parents. I was with Jahan and some others, watching old Nina Simone performances on YouTube. I nearly lost it. I had to run into the bathroom to calm down. Soraya's explanation, her logic that my parents were getting suspicious, that people were talking—it all slipped through my head like grains of sand.*

They knew.
They finally knew.

Interrogation Room 38

Soraya

I KNOW I *shouldn't have done that.*

That was so stupid of me to come out for Amir. It was like I wasn't even thinking. But my parents were looking at me so desperately, like they wanted to know more, like nothing I could say would stop them on their quest to find Amir.

They didn't believe me at first. They thought I had made it up. "No, no, no," they said. "That can't be true." So I doubled down and told them I had already talked to Amir about it and that I loved him, and I just got super mushy and defensive. I think my mom started to believe it first, because her lips became a straight line, kind of like they are now. They asked me to leave the kitchen.

I went up to my room and just sat there on my bed, feeling really, really bad. I texted Amir to tell him. He didn't text me back until much later. He just asked that if Maman and Baba were going to call him, that I be on the call.

The call didn't really go very well.

Interrogation Room 37

Amir

I'M NOT GOING *to talk about that phone call.*

Interrogation Room 39

Afshin Azadi

MY RELATIONSHIP WITH *Amir? My relationship with my son is fine. He has always been a very smart, responsible boy, a practical boy, so this running away episode is out of the ordinary. The episode on the plane is out of the ordinary. This is not the Amir I know.*

The Amir I know . . . I know my son is strong. But I worry for him in the other room, if you are questioning him right now. He is sensitive. He is—I don't want to say "broken" right now, but he is going through a lot, so you must take everything he says with a grain of salt.

You say if you had to guess, you think I'm going through a lot as well? I am fine, sir. I would not say this is ideal, but I am fine. I have everything under control. I am a man, and this is my family. Things might be difficult, not exactly the way I would have liked them to turn out, but I am fine.

These questions have nothing to do with why we were pulled aside on that plane. My family was just having a conversation. That was all.

Fifteen Days Ago

I DIPPED MY fingers in the fountain. I had spilled some prosecco on my shirt right before my parents called, before I clumsily picked up, and I figured I should try and wash it out.

"Where are you?" my dad asked over the phone. "Why do you keep ignoring our calls?"

"It doesn't matter," I said, dabbing the new shirt I bought yesterday. The store was called OVS; basically, the Italian T.J.Maxx.

"Amir," he said, exhausted. "Just come home."

"After that last call? No way," I said, standing up from the ledge of the marble fountain. I saw Jahan and the others out of the corner of my eye, on a bench at the edge of the park, opening another bottle of prosecco. I wanted to be back with them.

"Please. We can work on it together," my mom said. Those were the same words she used on our last call, the one that ended in fireworks. How long ago was that now? Four days? Five?

"*Work on it*," I spat into the phone.

"We can get you help," Dad said. "You're confused, we understand—"

"I'm not confused!" I yelled. I nearly knocked over a little Italian boy. "I already told you. I am not confused. I could not be less confused. There is not a single bone in my body that is confused."

"Yes, you are!"

"My dear son, please listen. Life is going to be harder. You're not—"

"One second," I said. I saw Jahan approaching, waving, his fingernails covered in black nail polish. *Is everything okay?* he mouthed. *It's fine*, I mouthed back. He nodded and turned around.

My heart was racing all of a sudden. Jahan and the others were looking at me suspiciously now. "I have to go," I said to my mom and dad.

I took a long, drawn-out breath, trying to wipe the anger off my face. I shouldn't have picked up the call, not after the last one. Great. Now I was all riled up again. It was like I had dropped a box labeled FRAGILE: HANDLE WITH CARE.

The whole time, I could picture exactly how it would go down if I went home. I didn't have to do the mental math anymore. I had read enough online forums to read between the lines when they said, "We can *work* on it."

There was no way I was leaving Italy at this point. Besides, I had a life here.

I was spending my days with Jahan. I'd found my own apartment in Testaccio, two blocks away from this park where he and his friends liked to drink prosecco during the day. I was also spending more time at Tiberino—the restaurant on Tiber Island—editing Wikipedia pages to make money.

I was a little nervous about money. I had finished the edits for that crypto start-up three days ago, and they still hadn't sent the money to my PayPal account.

But it was worth it. Late nights at Rigatteria, afternoons spent in Piazza Testaccio. Movies with Jahan and his friends in his living room, eighties music videos and clips from *RuPaul's Drag Race*.

I took one more breath and marched back over to Jahan and his friends on the bench. I liked this life. A lot.

Before I could even sit down, Rocco asked me, "What is the weirdest place where you have hooked up?"

"We're playing a game," Jahan explained, handing me a new plastic cup with prosecco. "Where we go around and each say the weirdest place where we've done the dirty deed. Or, at least, *some* deed."

I was still frazzled after that call with my parents. I took a sip of prosecco.

"Can you skip me?" I asked.

Rocco rolled his eyes. He was lying flat on the bench with his face toward the sky. Jahan, who was kneeling next to him with the prosecco bottle, opened his mouth to say something, but I interrupted.

"I guess a lot of times in the car," I said, sitting down next to Rocco's feet. "With this one guy, specifically. He went to my school."

"That is *so* American. And *so* high school," Rocco said. "I always forget you were in high school, like, yesterday."

"Was he your boyfriend?" Neil asked gently, his eyebrows raised.

I laughed. "Not really. I wasn't out, obviously, and neither was he, so we mostly just snuck around and hooked up."

Then I started smiling. "There was this one time, though. Jackson—that was his name—he and I decided to see a movie together. That was big for us. We didn't go to a movie theater in our town—we went to one in Springfield, this other town that was a little farther away, where we knew no one from our school would see us. It was a weeknight, and we were seeing *Jumanji*, the new one that came out at Christmastime. It had been out for a while, so we didn't think there would be a lot of people in the theater. But we were still nervous."

Jahan leaned forward, his elbows on the bench just inches from my waist. Rocco squinted his beady brown eyes. Neil smiled.

"The theater was practically empty, just like we expected. We sat in the back row, and after, I don't know, maybe fifteen minutes, we felt safe enough to hold hands. God, that might have even been our first real date, now that I think of it? But that's not the point. The point is, we were kissing and feeling each other up and stuff. I was so paranoid. It was my idea, because I just—I wanted to do something with Jackson that didn't involve a vehicle—but I was just freaking out the whole time."

"Did you fuck?" Rocco asked.

"Rocco, shut up," Neil hissed. "Keep going, Amir."

I nodded. "But then Jackson noticed something. He looked over across the aisle, and behind the last row, there was a space. Just a foot or two between the back of the seats and the wall. Enough space for two people to fit in."

"Oh my God," Rocco said, and Jahan nearly shoved him off the bench.

My heart was thumping faster. I took a breath. "Jackson looked over at that space, and my eyes followed, and we just stared at each other in the dark. I think we were thinking the same thing. All I wanted in that moment was Jackson, on a flat surface. Not a car seat, not a movie theater seat. So we went."

After the park, we stopped by Mercato Testaccio, a busy market with small stands and portly sellers that was filled to the brim with tourists. We had to pick up some ingredients for dinner—pasta and vegetables, meats and cheeses.

Jahan seemed to know all the vendors. Every time we went to pick something up, Jahan would chitchat with the person at the stand. They never wanted to let him pay. He'd pull out his wallet and the seller would wave their hands and it went back and forth like this until they finally took his money. It reminded me of the battle to pay the bill any time my family went out to dinner with another Iranian family. Soraya and I never understood why they couldn't just split it. I mean, we knew *why*, but still.

We went back to Jahan's apartment across the river to cook dinner together. Jahan had to run out and grab some wine, and Neil was preparing the salad in the other room, which meant I was stuck in the tiny kitchen with Rocco.

I started to rip the plastic wrapping off the pasta from the market. Rocco shook his head. "No, you have to boil the water first."

"I knew that," I said. I looked around the kitchen. I was still in a bit of a funk after the call with my parents. Rocco sighed audibly and bent down to get a pot from one of the cupboards.

"Here, fill this with water," Rocco said.

I took the pot and went to fill it up in the sink.

"That's enough," he said, turning the faucet off. Rocco reached under my arms and took the pot over to the gas stove. He twisted the knob. *Click, click, click,* fire.

I slid around him and started opening the can of pomodoro tomatoes on the counter. Rocco was watching me out of the side of his eye as I pulled the metal lid off.

"Do not spill the tomatoes," Rocco said to me. "Giovanni's cleaning lady had to spend an hour cleaning up the next day after you spilled those meatballs."

The water wasn't boiling yet, but my blood was. Ever since the night I rejected him, Rocco had been acting generally unpleasant around me, but tonight he was on another level. I wasn't in the mood for his shit.

"How are you and Giovanni doing?" I asked.

"We are *great*." Rocco snatched the can of tomatoes from in front of me and emptied it into a pan over the stove. "How are *you* doing?"

"I've been better," I said.

"I heard that you have an apartment in Testaccio. So you live here now?"

I shrugged. "I guess. I'm still not sure if I officially have the apartment. I didn't sign any papers. The landlord is a friend of Francesco's or something. I just paid him some money for rent and, like, some kind of deposit, and I got the keys. Is that normal?"

"In Italy, yes." Rocco picked up the olive oil jar and drizzled some onto the pan, but a few drops slid down the jar onto his white shirt. "*Cazzo!*" he screamed.

I got him a paper towel. "I'm sure Giovanni's cleaning lady can clean it," I said with a smirk. I couldn't resist.

Rocco shook his head. "It is not my shirt."

"Giovanni seems to have plenty of shirts, doesn't he? He'll be fine." I was confused. I thought Giovanni and Rocco were loaded. What did it matter if one shirt got ruined?

Rocco was about to say something, but he shut his mouth. "Yes, Giovanni has *many* shirts." He leaned against the counter and started dabbing the stain with the paper towel. Then he looked at me. "It is very random that you are here."

I *really* wasn't in the mood for his shit tonight. "I can leave if you'd like me to."

"I did not mean it like that," he said, as if what I proposed was ridiculous. "I meant in Rome. I would like to know a little bit more about you, where you came from. You are a stranger. I suppose that is how Jahan operates—he likes to bring in the strays—but I am just saying, it is random."

This, coming from an adult who makes art out of macaroni. Before I could say something I might regret, Neil squeezed into the kitchen. "Guys, this salad is going to be so good. Pear and arugula, with walnuts and shaved parmesan." He grabbed the salt and pepper shakers and a wooden spoon from the counter. "Oh, I overheard you guys talking from the other room, and I just gotta say, Rocco, not everyone was born in Rome like you. Some of us came from other places."

Rocco snatched the wooden spoon out of Neil's hand and stirred the tomato sauce. "Yes, but there is a difference between coming here from Milan because you could not make it as a model, and just showing up out of the blue like Amir."

"I did not go to Milan to *model*," Neil said, spitting out the word. "I went to Milan for a *boy*, then stumbled into modeling, and when both of those things busted, I came to Rome."

"Because that is what Rome needs," Rocco said. "More Americans."

"Do you have a problem with Americans?" I asked.

Rocco sighed. "I do not have any problems. I do not see why you believe I have any problems."

"Oh yeah, this guy doesn't have *any* problems," Neil laughed. "Where is Giovanni today, Rocco? Is he busy again?"

Rocco narrowed his eyes on Neil. "Yes, he is busy. We have our own lives. A wild concept. Love can be a disease when it is too intense, you know."

Now Neil was glaring back at Rocco. Suddenly, the door to the apartment clicked open and Jahan appeared. The kitchen was packed now. Jahan set the dark bottles of wine on the counter and looked at us, took a whiff, and frowned. I was positive he could smell the tension just as strongly as the tomato sauce.

"*Allora* . . ." Jahan said, getting between Neil and Rocco. "I haven't seen you two in such close quarters since—well, anyway. Neil, the salad is looking great, isn't it? You always make the most delicious salads."

Neil smiled and left the kitchen with the shakers.

Rocco exhaled. He seemed relieved to have Neil out of his hair. Jahan merrily threw an arm around Rocco's shoulder.

"Remember that amazing Bolognese your mother used to make for us, Rocco? I still have dreams about that Bolognese. Creamy, saucy, delicious dreams." Jahan looked over at the pot of water on the stove. "I trust this pasta will be right up there, won't it?"

Then he turned to me. "Hey, Amir. The water is boiling."

Fourteen Days Ago

IT WAS A cool Italian night, the stars in full view over the rooftop of Rigatteria. Broken windowpanes and antique furniture were scattered all over the giant wooden deck. At my last Italian lesson, Francesco explained to me—through Neil, who translated his broken English—that Rigatteria was actually built on the side of a mound called Monte Testaccio, which used to be where ancient Romans all disposed of their olive oil jars. We were partying atop millions of broken antique shards.

About fifteen people were taking turns breaking a piñata when I arrived. I'm not going to describe the piñata in detail, except to say that it was exceptionally phallic.

Meanwhile, Jahan was trying to convince a group of Italians that gorgonzola is the gayest cheese.

"*Ascoltami,*" he said. He noticed me out of the side of his eye. "*Sembra che tu stia succhiando un cazzo quando lo dici.* Gorrrrgonnnzzzoollllaaaaa," he stretched out the word and made a sexual gesture with his hand and mouth.

"Gorrgonnzoolaaa," one of the boys said.

"Gorrggohhrrrhgghhh," said a girl with pink streaks in her hair. She practically choked on the word. Jahan explained to me what was going on, and I agreed that although I might have previously questioned how cheese could have a sexual orientation, after this debate, I fully believed that gorgonzola was the gayest cheese.

I looked around for Neil and Francesco. Between the penis piñata and the gorgonzola debate, it didn't seem like quite the right mood for a proposal tonight. Though I should have been used to these gay blends of silly and serious. It seemed to be the tempo of my life these days.

After the candy and condoms from the penis piñata had been cleared out, Francesco stepped out from behind the bar. Everyone gathered around him.

Francesco spoke in Italian—fast, nervous, shaky—but I didn't need any translation when he got down on one knee. The way he looked in Neil's eyes when he popped the question, the way Neil held his hand over his chest as he watched, and the way he uttered one of the few words in Italian I knew—si—I was overwhelmed. We all were.

Everyone pulled out their phones to take pictures. I would have pulled mine out, too, but the camera was hardly any good. I was using an old Android Jahan had given me earlier that day. After the last call with my parents, I decided to lose my American number and get an Italian one. I didn't share that number with anyone from back home.

As Jahan and Neil and Francesco, all their friends, their family, snapped photos and cheered, something came over me. I was so damn happy for Neil and Francesco. I thought maybe someday, I could find happiness, too.

Later, I found Neil in the crowd. He slung an arm around my neck and I went in for a full hug, like we were best friends or something. Neil stumbled forward; he was more than a little bit drunk. I held him up. High on the proposal, on the energy of the moment, I said, *"Auguri"*—the Swiss Army knife of Italian words, which has many different uses, but in this case, *congratulations*. He smiled.

"You've been studying," Neil said.

"I have," I said, and I couldn't believe I was having this conversation, this close to Neil, this soon after he had just been proposed to.

It must have felt that way for Neil, too. "Thanks, man," he said. "I expect to see you at the wedding, you know."

I pulled back from the hug, my face dumbstruck. I was hung up on the fact that Neil, the hot tutor of my dreams, had invited me to his wedding. And I wasn't the least bit heartbroken. It didn't ruin the fantasy at all. There was no fantasy. Friendship, I realized, is better than fantasy.

I was riding higher and higher. The strings of light around the rooftop glowed warmly. More people began to fill the space and dance. Love was in the air.

Glow sticks were in the air, too. Jahan had gone downstairs and came back with a whole box of them. He'd crack a bundle of glow sticks and shake vigorously before he tossed them, lighting up the sky like fireworks.

I caught a glow stick and ambled my way downstairs to the

bathroom. I was sober, but I felt drunker than I'd ever been.

The basement had to be negative eight million degrees Celsius—Celsius!—but I still felt warm and boozy inside. Even with the long line at the bathroom, my priority was not to relieve my bladder but to create a glow stick bracelet by poking the end of the glow stick into the little plastic fastener thingy. Even in my relatively sober state, I was hard-core struggling to fasten the glow stick around my wrist.

And then I heard, "Here, let me help you. You need two people for that."

Behind me, a boy with curly brown hair offered a hand. He looked extremely tall, but that was because he was standing a step above me. When he came down, he was only a couple of inches taller than me. Droopy, kind eyes. The kind that look tired in a cute way. He took one end of the glow stick while I held the plastic fastener, and when he pushed it in, his thumb pressed into my wrist.

"There," he said.

"Thanks," I said back.

I was going to introduce myself, do more than just stand there and give the tile floor a dumb smile, but the bathroom freed up. So I went inside. When I came out, he was gone, so I went back upstairs.

I rejoined Jahan and Giovanni and Rocco on the dance floor. I noticed glow stick bathroom boy sitting at a small table by the bar.

"Who's that?" I asked Jahan over the music; it was poppy and Italian, and everyone was singing along.

"That's Valerio," Jahan said. "He's Francesco's cousin. I think he's a student or something in Rome. Looks like he's working the drink ticket booth." He prodded me with his elbow. "Are you interested, Amir?"

I didn't say anything, but I did decide I needed a drink.

My heart was beating fast, again, just like in the basement, as I walked up to the drinks booth. He, Valerio—who had not introduced himself to me yet, and for all I knew now, maybe wasn't flirting in the basement but genuinely just wanted to help me put my glow stick on—was standing in front of a small table with a metal cash box. He, Valerio—the first boy I would ever make a move on in my life, since technically Jackson had approached me—was talking to an extremely attractive Italian girl. He, Valerio—descendant of Julius Caesar and Michelangelo and Al Pacino and—

All right, you get the picture. I was nervous. There was a lot going through my head.

But then Valerio did something drastic, something that would relieve all the fear swirling in my head: He looked away from the intensely spray-tanned Italian girl, looked over at me, and smiled.

Valerio ripped a red ticket from the ticket wheel and held it under the table. His eyes flickered downward. The girl laughed and said something in Italian, glancing over at me. It struck me that they were both waiting for me to take the ticket.

I shook my head and took it. At the bar, I ordered an Aperol spritz, which tasted refreshingly sweet.

Someone tapped my shoulder. "Hello, bathroom boy."

I turned around, but Valerio had slunk around next to me at the bar. He barely had an Italian accent. "Thanks for the f-free drink," I said.

"It is my pleasure," he said, and okay, now he had an accent. Or was he trying really hard to sound like he didn't have one?

"How did you know I didn't speak Italian?" I asked.

"Because you would yell 'damn it!' every time you could not get that bracelet on," Valerio said. God, his eyes were cute. Bluish green.

I turned red.

"Aren't you going to ask my name?" he asked.

"Umm," I said, taking a big sip of my drink.

"Valerio."

"Amir," I said. Behind him, Giovanni was ordering a drink at the bar. He winked at me.

"So . . . you sell drink tickets?" I asked Valerio.

"Yes, but my shift is over."

"I don't see anyone else manning the ticket table," I said. "Does that mean the drinks are free now?"

"For me, I hope so. God knows I cannot afford them," Valerio said.

"With a job like that, I'd assume you were loaded."

Valerio nudged me with his elbow. "I work four jobs like that, at other bars and restaurants in Testaccio, and I am still not, as you say, 'loaded.'"

It turned out Valerio was a student at Sapienza University in

Rome. He had just finished his freshman year, and he was studying the very lucrative field of Latin.

"So you're a nerd," I said.

"I am actually very dumb."

"I bet if I looked up this school right now, it's probably the best college in Italy."

Valerio scratched the back of his head, and I immediately pulled out my phone. He tried to take it away from me, but I managed to pull up the Wikipedia page.

"See!" I yelled, twisting my body to keep him away from my phone. "It says right here, 'one of the most prestigious Italian universities, commonly ranking first'—"

"Okay, okay," Valerio said, giggling. I looked back and saw Jahan and the others watching our little tug-of-phone.

After the bar shut down, Valerio suggested we continue our conversation over on a couch in the corner. Where our hips touched. And then our legs became intertwined. The dance floor was sparse, and it was at least five in the morning.

"I should get going," Valerio said. "But I like you. You are funny. Let me get your number."

I gave it to him. We didn't kiss, although that might have been my fault, because I got sidetracked when I saw that my friends were retreating downstairs.

I said goodbye to Valerio and ran down the stairs, into the room of Italian antiques, where they had taken refuge on a couch in the very back of the center room—it felt like a ship cabin, with high ceilings, curved, just extremely deep. Neil was popping a bottle of prosecco and Jahan was going through a record collection in a dusty cabinet to the side of the couches.

"Whitney Houston!" Jahan yelped.

"Madonna!" Neil cheered as he uncorked the bottle.

He poured the prosecco into a line of flutes for us, and we toasted to the night.

Interrogation Room 38

Soraya

I NEEDED TO *know where Amir had gone. I had already messed everything up by telling my mom and dad. Amir must have blocked us or something, because after a few days of nonstop calls—nonstop yelling— he stopped picking up our calls. They stopped going through. They would just go straight to voicemail.*

Eleven Days Ago

WHEN I RANG the doorbell, I could hear dogs barking in the background and Neil yelling over them. "Mina! Firenze! *Calmatevi!*"

The lock rustled. "One second," Neil said. He cracked the door open, the dogs skittering around his feet. "Hey! Come in," he said.

We were having our lesson at Neil's apartment today because I wanted to meet his dogs. I had thought he would just bring them by Rigatteria, but Neil had the day off from the bookstore, so he asked if I could just meet him at his apartment.

Neil and Francesco lived in a neighborhood called Pigneto (pronounced pin-yeto; in our first lesson, Neil had told me that in Italian, you pronounce every letter. I soon learned that was a big lie). I got there by taking one of the trams from Trastevere to Porta Maggiore, a massive, ancient gate that used to be part of the wall of Rome and was now a major traffic hub.

Neil's apartment was much nicer than Jahan's. It was airy, with a large balcony and lots of antique art scattered throughout. We studied on the couch in the living room, our notebooks spread out over the treasure chest coffee table. The couch was old and sank, which meant his waist was pressed right into mine and our knees sometimes touched. But I wasn't freaking out nearly as much as you might expect. Just weeks ago, if you'd typed this equation into the Hot Dude Calculator—hidden heartthrob, works at a bookstore, multiplied by intimate Italian lessons—you would have gotten ERROR: CANNOT COMPUTE. Divided by a lesson at his apartment? LOL: GOOD ONE.

But today, I was fine. I kept my cool. Besides, I had a date with Valerio tonight. A real date. My very first real date. He had asked after that night at Rigatteria if he could take me out to dinner.

When I told Neil, he became unreasonably excited. "We found you an Italian boy!" he exclaimed. Even the dogs were freaking out. Neil translated what I had just told him for Francesco, and midsentence, Francesco's eyebrows shot up, but then he smiled. He said something in Italian. "Keeping it in the family," Neil translated for me.

We spent the rest of the lesson going over Italian words for love and bed-related things. Francesco got involved. They were like my gay uncles, preparing me for my very first date.

On my way out the door, Neil taught me one more phrase, "*In bocca al lupo*," he said, patting me on the shoulder. "It means good luck. Although—Italian has a lot of weird phrases like this—it technically translates into, 'in the mouth of the wolf.' You're supposed to respond '*crepi*,' which basically means, 'may the wolf die.'"

I shook my head. "Italian is a strange language."

Outside, I found Valerio leaning against a motorcycle. I complimented him on finding such a badass vehicle to stand and look cool against, and he chuckled and said, "No, this is mine."

I gawked for a second. "I'm not getting on that," I said.

Valerio frowned. "Come on, it is safe! I have been riding it since I was your age."

"So you've been riding it for two years. Nuh-uh. I'm not getting on a motorcycle."

"It is a scooter."

"When you said you'd pick me up, I thought you meant by foot, or maybe, at best, with a car . . ."

"I did not specify what kind of ride," he said, smiling. I don't know if he meant it that way, but I couldn't help thinking about that line sexually. *What kind of ride.* And that was all it took for me to get on his motorcycle-scooter thing. God, I'm easy.

Valerio gestured at the handlebars below the passenger seat. "You can hold tight to these handles down here, or you can hold tight to me."

"Well, that's one way to make a move," I said.

I strapped on my helmet. Valerio accelerated smoothly down the street. My nerves calmed; this didn't feel so different from driving a car. Until, *whoa*, the first turn felt like we were karate chopping through the air. So I gripped his waist tighter.

We sliced through the highway. Every time we hit a bump, I gripped my fingers tighter around Valerio's waist, and he laughed. The wind whipped my T-shirt. "I hope that thing doesn't fly off," Valerio said. He was talking! Like it was a normal car ride and we were just two normal passengers.

Valerio parked the motorcycle—I mean, *scooter*—and I dismounted awkwardly, one leg stuck in the air like I was contemplating a drop kick. My legs were shaking as they touched the ground.

I took off the helmet, and Valerio laughed. "You were supposed to buckle up," he said.

"What? There was no seat belt," I said, pointing at the seat. "I thought *you* were my seat belt."

"I mean the helmet," he said. "You never buckled it. I was going slowly, so it stayed on your head. But if I had gone any faster, it would have definitely flown off."

I had a hard time believing that *that* was slow, but I smiled at the possibility of maybe someday going faster with Valerio.

Valerio took me to an outdoor restaurant in Garbatella, a sort of quaint Italian neighborhood not too far from bustling Trastevere. There were actual houses there—not unlike the colonial homes in Maryland, where I grew up—with yards and front doors and mailboxes. They were more colorful, though. Less brick, more color. That's how I would sum up Roman architecture, if I had to.

He ordered for us as soon as we sat down, a long string of Italian peppered with words I recognized like "spaghetti" and "bruschetta" and "tiramisu." I asked Valerio if this was where he brought all the American boys he picked up at two in the morning. That led to him telling me about his first and only relationship, with an upperclassman he had met his third week of college.

"I thought he was my *amore*," Valerio said, he said, taking a last bite of our *primi*, the pasta dish. It was the most delicious red-sauced pasta I've had in my life. "I was not expecting the breakup. I was extremely heartbroken."

I assumed this meant that Valerio was still a virgin, like me, until he told me about the aftermath.

"I am very sensitive when the people I like disappear. It is the Italian in me. We are very emotional." He paused. "You could say I am scarred."

"In America we call that ghosting," I said.

"Yes, I am afraid of ghosts." Valerio chuckled, probably pleased with himself that he'd made a dating/Halloween crossover joke. But then his face got grim. "After my *amore* and I broke up, he stopped talking to me. And so I went out with my friends that Friday night. I met a boy who quite literally swept me off my feet. He marched up to me at the bar, and I thought there was someone attractive behind me, so I turned around. But he wanted me. He said, '*Un bel ragazzo*'—beautiful man—with such confidence."

The waiter stopped by and dropped off our *secondi*. Valerio said "*grazie*" and gestured at me to take a bite, and over a thin slice of veal that melted in my mouth, I asked him to keep telling the story.

"Oh, he was beautiful himself," Valerio said, his eyes lost in the past. "Beach-blond hair, tall, tan like a Sicilian. I could not have drawn up a more attractive man. Within minutes we were kissing. My friends left me with this boy. I believe his name was Alessio. I will spare you the details, except that on our way to his apartment just blocks away from the bar, he bought a rose for me from one of those gypsy street peddlers. A rose! And so in my drunken, heartbroken state that night, I slept with him. He was gentle. So kind. The next morning, I walked home from his apartment, happier than I had ever been with my *amore*. I felt hope. I felt wanted.

I knew where this story was headed, and my face turned grim as well. "He never texted you," I said. "Did he?"

Valerio's eyes fell to the table. "He did not. Another ghost. It truly hurt."

I took a long sip of red wine. I couldn't help but think about Jackson, how I might have hurt him in the same way when I just cut him off like that.

"I'm sorry, Valerio," I said.

"It is fine," he said, and he raised his glass to me. "Nothing a little wine cannot help."

"*Salute*," I said.

"Cheers," he said, exhaling.

Dessert was sweet and soft and cocoa-filled. The lights strewn around the outdoor restaurant grew brighter. We stumbled off back to Valerio's motorcycle—at least, I did. Valerio only had one glass; I finished the bottle. I assumed this was the end of the night, but Valerio drove past my neighborhood and up and up a winding road until we reached the most amazing view of Rome.

It was an area like a piazza—a *piazzale*, Valerio called it—high up, like an outdoor observatory. Hordes of other people, mostly around our age, hung around the ledges, drinking and taking in the view.

"*Piazzale*," I said, stretching the word. "Like a piazza but high up?"

Valerio thought for a moment. "Not quite. A piazza is surrounded by buildings on every side. A *piazzale* usually has a side that is not buildings," he said, sweeping his hand across the view.

"So it's like a peninsula," I said.

"What?"

"An island is surrounded by water on all sides," I said. "But a peninsula has one side that's connected to land."

Valerio still looked confused. "It is not a peninsula. It is a *piazzale*."

I snorted. "You're a *piazzale*."

He shrugged. "If you insist."

We claimed a space on the stone ledge, and he called out some of Rome's wonders from the skyline: Saint Peter's Basilica, the Colosseum, the Roman Forum, and, next to it, the two-thousand-year-old chariot racing track.

"My friends from Rome, they say they used to drink and make out there when they were in high school," Valerio told me.

"Where I'm from," I said, "people in high school drink and make out in dark parks, not on ancient Roman racing tracks."

Valerio giggled, scooting closer to me on the ledge. He leaned in and whispered, "I would make out with you anywhere. Racing track, dark park, wherever," he said, his warm breath tickling my ear.

I pulled back.

"What is wrong?" Valerio asked.

I looked around the *piazzale* nervously. There were so many people around, most of them straight couples, though there were two girls who looked like they could be together. "Nothing, nothing," I said, forcing a smile.

Valerio and I sat and talked for a while, and then he drove me back to my place, the ride even scarier and more life-threatening in the dark. He helped me off the scooter.

"Do you live alone?" he asked.

"Yeah," I said, "though I kind of miss living with Jahan. I was on his couch for a few days when I first came to Rome."

"That is really nice of Jahan," Valerio said, swinging his arms.

"He's been so great to me," I said, swinging mine. "He—" Before I could finish my sentence, Valerio grabbed my elbows and pulled me in and pressed his lips against mine.

I stood still.

I must have look petrified, because Valerio's face fell. It was just like that split second in the car with Jackson, the first time we kissed, when I pulled back. Valerio started to stutter that he should go.

"No," I pleaded. "Sorry."

"Why are you sorry?" he asked, confused.

Something about being boozy and having my own place made me wonder the same thing. Why *was* I sorry?

"Do you want to come up?" I asked, half smiling.

Valerio paused, looked at me, completed my smile, and nodded.

I fumbled with my giant key until I got it in the keyhole. That's not an innuendo. That's just a statement of fact. Then we cannonballed onto my bed. Fact. Valerio kissed me like a skilled sailor tying the most perfect knot in the middle of the ocean. Subjective, non-fact.

Valerio took off his shirt. Fact. There was a shiny silver pin punctured through his right nipple. Fact.

Remember Jahan's nipple story? The one I've alluded to but have been waiting for the right moment to tell?

We have arrived. Our destination is on the right.

When I caught sight of Valerio's shiny piercing, my mind immediately raced through Jahan's story: His friend had gone home with a cool DJ, tattoos and piercings and all, and they took off their clothes, and one of his nipples was pierced, so he went in and sucked the nipple, because that's what one does, apparently, and he enjoyed it, so he kept sucking. Then he felt something on his tongue, so he pulled back—*it's just a hair, bound to happen.* But when he checked his tongue, nothing was there, and then he noticed something dangling from the guy's pink little pepperoni, a white string. That was when it hit him.

He had sucked the nerve tendon out of his crush's nipple.

When the cool DJ saw it for himself, he was just like, "Oh yeah, that happens all the time." So he just pushed.

It.

Back.

In.

The whole story flashed through my head, with Valerio on my bed, shirtless. It was like a movie montage.

"What is it?" he said, staring at me.

I shook my face. "Nothing."

Valerio and I made out a bit longer. I avoided his chest area altogether, focusing on the waist just like I had done on his motorscoodoodle. At one point, Valerio ran his fingers gently through my hair, and that small act reminded me of Jackson— how he used to do the same thing, and I would do it to him. How I'd sometimes find strands of his blond hair on my sweatshirt and smile.

Moments later, I fell asleep.

Interrogation Room 38

Soraya

AMIR MIGHT HAVE *fought with my parents on the phone, but I was the one sparring with them in person. After those phone calls, I would pick up where Amir left off and fight with my parents, defending Amir. It was a lot of yelling. It was exhausting. Between the drama at Cats rehearsal and the drama at home, I was getting tired.*

I kept looking for Amir. I went back to Jake in the mall. I kept going back almost every day. One day I just snapped. "Seriously, it's sad how you're here every day," I said angrily to him. "Is this what you're going to do with the rest of your life?"

Jake was visibly hurt. "If Amir had just given me the money, I wouldn't effing be here." I can't really repeat the word he used in front of my mom, but just know that my face looked pretty much like hers does right now.

I realized this stupid kid had blackmailed my brother. He tried to come up with excuses in front of me—if Amir had just given him the money, Jake could have afforded community college, and Amir's secret would have stayed safe, and they both would have been better off—but I shook my head. "You're a coward," I told him.

I wanted to storm off, but I stayed. Jake might know something, I thought. I asked him why in the world he would think my brother made money off of Wikipedia pages, and Jake said he saw Amir editing a page back in the fall. I asked, "What about Jackson? Did you blackmail him, too?" Jake looked at me like I was insane. He went on about how the Preachers were good people and did lots of good things for the community. I rolled my eyes. "You won't exploit the Preachers, but you'll exploit the new Muslim kid," I said. "Nice one."

At this point I was really ready to leave when I asked Jake one more thing: "What page was Amir editing?" Jake laughed and said it was the Real Housewives of New Jersey page. I asked him why he was laughing, and he said no, don't worry about it, and I said no, tell me. He said he and Ben liked to joke that they should have known Amir was gay when they caught him editing that page. I told Jake he was an idiot and to fuck off.

Language. Sorry, Mom.

When I got home, I jumped on the computer and looked at the edit history for the Real Housewives of New Jersey page for back in the fall. I found my brother's Wikipedia username. He'd been editing pages as recently as yesterday. He had edited multiple pages in Rome.

Ten Days Ago

I WAS MORTIFIED when we woke up in the morning.

"I mean it, do not worry," Valerio insisted.

"But I fell asleep while we were kissing," I groaned, wiping the sleep out of my eyes. My face felt heavy, my head cloudy. Meanwhile, Valerio was just lying there on his side, looking perfect. "I just—uggghh."

Valerio leaned in and kissed me on the forehead. "It happens," he said. His lips brought my face back to life. Lips like that cured diseases. Lips like that were an art form. Lips like that deserved full, undivided attention.

"I was so tired," I said. "And so full."

"Blame it on the Italian food, yes."

"It's true! How are people expected to hook up after an Italian meal?" I raised my voice, letting out a violent cough. Valerio looked at me, amused. "I mean, there's the *antipasti*, the *primi*, the *secondi*, and then, as if all those courses weren't enough, *dolci*. Plus, there's all that wine. Of course I'm going to pass out."

"So what you are saying is . . . it is not me, it is the pasta?" Valerio teased.

"Valerio." I gave him a very serious look. "I'm sorry, but this isn't working." I put a hand on his shoulder. "It's not you. It's the pasta." I snorted, and we both burst out laughing. We rolled around in bed for a while, and then Valerio got dressed and left.

Jahan had left me two voice memos on WhatsApp last night. The first one was while I was at dinner with Valerio. *"Amir agha, I can't remember if your date was tonight or tomorrow? Hold on, one second. I have to go. We're splashing around in the fountain in Piazza Testaccio, and it looks like a Carabiniere is approaching. Maybe he wants to join the fun, maybe he wants to arrest us . . . you never know!"*

I nearly spat out my water. And then a few hours later, *"All right. We're fine. No one got arrested. So I can only assume you're on your date right now. I hope it's going splendidly. I just wanted to remind you that you promised you'll read something at Garbo tomorrow night. No excuses!"*

Right. I did promise him that. This would be Jahan's last reading at Garbo, after nearly four years of hosting them. It was a bleak reminder that he would be leaving Rome in less than two weeks. In two weeks, there would be no one to convince us to drink prosecco in the afternoon, no one to spread the gospel of Joni Mitchell, no one to determine which cheeses were gay, straight, or asexual.

What would Rome be without Jahan?

I went to Tiberino to try and write something for tonight. Mr. Pedrotti brought me a glazed apple pastry, which was delicious and sweet but did nothing to get my creative juices flowing. I wanted to pull my hair out. I didn't have a creative bone in my body. I preferred sticking to the facts on Wikipedia—hard, citable facts.

Suddenly a shadowy figure appeared over my notebook. I looked up. It was a girl, and she had short hair, almost a buzz cut, and an extremely angular face.

"Whoa! I know you!" I said.

It was Laura Pedrotti.

Laura dumped her shoulder bag on the table, nearly knocking off my laptop, and sat down. She kicked up her feet.

"You look just like your pictures," I said.

Laura folded her arms. "Oh, *do* I?"

"I didn't mean it like that," I stammered. "You're just—you're very pretty."

"Oh, please, *go on*," she said, sweeping her hands. "I love nothing more than to be objectified, especially when it's by the nerd who made my Wikipedia page."

"No, no, I'm not objectifying you. I'm actually—"

"I'm just playing with you," Laura said. She had a very tiny accent, though she sounded more American than anyone else I'd met in Rome. "Thank you for that page. I don't want to sound like a narcissist and say I appreciate it, but . . . I appreciate it. So my dad tells me you're struggling to write a poem? Is this for a class or something?"

"He told you that?"

She showed me the texts, which were in Italian but loosely translated to BOY WHO WROTE YOUR WIKIPEDIA PAGE IS TRYING TO WRITE A POEM, YOU ARE BEAUTIFUL WRITER, PERHAPS MY BEAUTIFUL DAUGHTER COULD DO FAVOR FOR THIS POOR AMERICAN.

"Trust me," Laura said, "his texts are even more ridiculous when I'm at school. He gets a little carried away when he texts. He's convinced I inherited his way with words. You can put that on the Wikipedia page." She winked.

Oh my God.

Was she flirting with me?

Did Laura Pedrotti want to get with the creator of her Wikipedia page?

"Thankfully he doesn't have my girlfriend's number," Laura continued, "so she is not victim to his texts. Yet."

I smiled. "I didn't read online that you have a girlfriend. I'll have to add that to your Personal Life section." Laura's face turned slightly horrified. "Just kidding," I quickly blurted. "I can't add anything without a citable source. Anyway. This poem."

"This poem," she repeated.

"I need inspiration."

Laura laughed and took a cigarette out of her bag. She flicked the lighter and gestured toward the church.

"See that church over there? It's called la Basilica di San Bartolomeo. The Basilica of Saint Bartholomew. The guy got skinned alive and beheaded. A lot of times when he is depicted in statues, you will find him holding his own skin, his body skinless, just veins and raw flesh."

"Gah!" I gagged, making a retching sound. "That's not inspiration! That's blatant torture!"

Laura smiled. "Made you feel something, didn't it?" She shook her head. "Just write something personal. From the heart. Put yourself out there and make yourself vulnerable . . . vulnerable as fuck." She had a point; after her Nespresso commercial song, Laura's second most popular song was a subtle-but-not-really ode to periods. She said in an interview that she hated how women weren't supposed to talk about them.

"Vulnerable," I said. "Got it."

"Vulnerable as fuck. *Raw.* Like Bartholomew."

This time Laura clapped her own hands over her mouth in disgust and made a sound. We laughed.

"Do you want to come to the reading tonight?" I asked. "It's at this bar, Garbo. You could sing something—"

"I'm good," Laura said. "I have plans with friends."

"Okay," I said.

"I appreciate the invite," she said, raising her chin. "And I'm a bit impressed? The American inviting the Italian girl to a party in her own town. You're already hanging out with the artsy crowd."

"Trust me," I said. "It doesn't feel real to me, either."

"I bet. Good luck with the reading," Laura said. "*In bocca al lupo.* You're supposed to respond—"

"*Crepi*," I said.

Laura looked even more impressed now. "Someone learns quickly," she said with a flick of her wrist.

My nerves kicked in as soon as I stepped into Garbo. I squeezed through crowds of people, swirls of Italian and English and French being spoken around me, and found Jahan exactly where I expected to find him, at the bar.

"I like the outfit," I said when I managed to squeeze between two people. Jahan was wearing a vest with little gold flowers and vines on it.

"Of course you do," Jahan said, cracking open a metal shaker. "It's from the Safavid/Qajar era. My favorite dynasties. They had their hands full fighting the Ottomans, and they *still* had time for fashion."

"Damn. Repping the squad," I said.

"Squad goals," Jahan said ironically, and I raised my hand for a high five, because he had actually remembered something I had taught him.

+20: Indoctrinate Jahan and his friends with pop culture references and other millennial theology.

Jahan topped the drink he was pouring with a lime wedge and passed it to a woman down the bar. "So do you know what you're reading tonight?"

I pulled out a folded sheet of paper from my pocket. In the end, I wasn't able to come up with anything on my own, but I found a really beautiful Rumi poem in a book Jahan gave me the other day.

"It's a surprise," I said. "But I think you'll like it."

Promptly at eleven thirty—a first in Garbo history, from what I understood of these weekly readings, and of Italian and Iranian culture in general—Jahan stood up and introduced the evening.

"Thank you everyone for coming tonight. I'm going to try not to cry. Not because I'm a man—fuck that—but because I don't want to ruin this gorgeous Persian vest I have on." Jahan flapped the vest and gave it a twirl, and everyone clapped and cheered. "You know, I wore this vest because I wanted to honor the Persian tradition of oral storytelling. We Persians, we can't just write stories like everyone else. We have to tell them out loud, epic and dramatic, much like we've been doing in this little bar for several years now. Thank you for indulging me in that tradition. I'm going to miss it."

And so the night began. People read stories. They read poetry. They put on fake accents and galloped like horses and made the room burst into laughter. It was a night for the books. The room was floating, and Jahan was on cloud nine.

He squirmed every time one of the presenters thanked him for Garbo. For the gift of this bar, these reading nights, his presence. Some people read poetry for Jahan: an Edward Lear limerick, a Shakespeare sonnet, a Rumi quatrain.

Then someone else read Rumi. And another person. Jahan quipped, "What's with all the Rumi tonight? A bitch loves her mystic Sufi poet, but how about some Hafiz or Saadi, people . . ."

I gulped.

Gaetano, a boy with bright red cheeks whom I hadn't really talked to much, stepped up to the front of the room. Instead of reading, he talked about how he had struggled to come out just two years ago. He spoke in Italian, but one of Jahan's friends translated into my ear.

"I used to come to Garbo . . . and drink alone in that corner over there . . . If at any point in the night, someone 'obviously gay' entered the bar, I would leave . . . I was not comfortable in my own skin . . . let alone in a bar like this."

Gaetano paused to make eye contact with Jahan. "One evening, Jahan approached me . . . 'Come sit at the bar,' he said . . . he was very obviously gay . . . such a fruit, so flamboyant . . . but there was something about him . . . something genuine . . . I joined him, and very quickly, he won me over . . . he was magic and laughter . . . the kind of presence that made you feel special . . . at that time, my own family was having trouble accepting me . . . I was angry, hateful, most of all, I hated myself . . . but Jahan, you saved me . . . It was because of you . . . I was able to accept myself after the people I loved could not . . . We will miss you."

Tears welled up in Jahan's eyes. He nodded at Gaetano, mouthed, *Thank you*, and called up the next presenter.

The next presenter was me.

I felt my heart thumping. Was it excitement? Was it nerves? I stood up slowly as Jahan introduced me. "Our next reader—he's only been in our lives for a couple of weeks, but it feels like we've known him forever."

The room was golden. It was glowing honey yellow, nectarine

orange, the warmest, most inviting colors. I melted into the whole thing. Everyone looked at me so welcomingly, and I felt at home.

"Ciao. My name is Amir." I took the sheet of paper out of my pocket and unfolded it slowly. "A lot of you don't know me. I ended up in Rome by accident, in a way, and became friends with Jahan and Neil, and all the others. They've been the nicest people in the world to me. I'm really thankful for that."

My hands were shaking. I couldn't believe how many people were packed into this bar, listening to me.

"It really is a tribute to what an incredible person Jahan is," I continued, "that we all get to be in this room tonight. Together. We could have been complete strangers, you know? We could have been standing behind one another in line at a bus stop. Or on a plane, filling the rows and seats, watching in-flight movies over one another's shoulders. We could have never met. But tonight, we get to meet. Because of Jahan."

My sweaty fingers clenched the poem I had yet to read. "You know, I just realized something," I said. "I think, someday in the future, I'll romanticize this moment. Standing in front of all of you. I won't remember the sweat dripping down the back of my neck. I won't remember how nervous I got each time Jahan called another presenter, thinking it would be my turn. I won't dock points for those little things, even if they meant something at the time, because I don't want them to define a beautiful moment. Life's not about keeping score like that. It's just not. It's about finding people who see you—because the minute they do, everything else goes away. All the points even out."

Suddenly, the room filled with applause. I looked over at Jahan, who nodded at me. I was still holding the Rumi poem in my hands. I folded it back up and put it into my pocket, and I went and sat down.

"That was a hell of a speech, Amir."

Giovanni had asked if I wanted to go outside for a smoke. I didn't, but I did want to go outside for some air, so I joined him.

"Thanks," I said, leaning against a motorcycle. "Where's Jahan?"

"Oh, he is going to be in very high demand tonight."

Giovanni took out a lighter and flicked the wheel, bringing the flame close to his cigarette. He took a deep drag. "I am going to miss him," he said.

I shoved my hands in my pockets. "So am I," I said. The cigarette glowed in the darkness, lighting up Giovanni's face like a Halloween jack-o'-lantern. I had always liked Giovanni, ever since he gave me that shirt at the first dinner party.

We talked about his novel, which Giovanni had been working on for years, and he droned on about fifteenth- and sixteenth-century queer Italian history for so long I lost track of time. I told him I wanted to read his book. Giovanni smiled, eyeing me with the precision of a hawk, and he said I could read it as soon as it was finished.

"I have not even shared it with Jahan yet," Giovanni said, taking another drag of his cigarette. "It is a shame we are losing him."

"You're telling me. He's pretty much the only person I have here," I said.

Giovanni frowned. "Stick with me and we will suffer through this loss together," he said. "In fact, a few of us are going up to my house in Umbria next week, right after Jahan's last day. It is a beautiful part of Italy, lush and hilly. My family has a villa there. You should come with us."

"Really? Would that be okay?"

"Of course."

Someone from the bar came out and asked us to come back inside. Apparently, the neighbors upstairs were complaining about the noise.

"Maybe my life won't be over after Jahan leaves," I said to Giovanni on our way in.

"Of course it will not. You will start a new life. A *new* new life. I am an expert in new lives. I have had a couple of them myself," he said with a wink, "and I am intrigued by yours."

Interrogation Room 38

Soraya

ONE OF THE pages Amir had edited on Wikipedia was for a singer named Laura Pedrotti. He had also edited some pages for a neighborhood called Trastevere. He had added a couple of locations to the page—a park, a bar—and I cross-checked those on Instagram to see if anyone had posted a picture of him or something.

That was when I found him. One of the locations, a bar called Garbo, had an active Instagram story. I tapped through the story, which showed a crowded room with people reading at the front, and there he was. Amir, wearing a white T-shirt and khaki pants, his hair long and black and curly, talking in front of a group of Italian people. He looked so confident up there. He was glowing under the bright lights.

Most of all, Amir looked happy—I could tell, even from that ten-second clip, that he was happier than I'd seen him in a long time.

Did I really want to ruin that?

Interrogation Room 38

Roya Azadi

GROWING UP, THERE *was a boy who lived on my block in Tehran. His name was Payman. He fluttered around our little street like a butterfly, always smiling, singing—like there was a world of happiness in every step he took. The other girls and I liked him. He wasn't threatening. But the boys constantly mocked him. Whenever we played with Payman, the boys would find us, and they would come over, cocky and stupid, just like most boys at that age, and they would tease Payman for no reason.* Che mikoni, parvaneh? *What are you doing, butterfly? They were so cruel to him.*

I haven't thought about Payman in a long time. His family left Tehran for the countryside; I don't know what happened to him, but later in life, I figured out why he was different. I figured out why those boys had teased him.

I don't want Amir to be different because I don't want him to get hurt.

Interrogation Room 39

Afshin Azadi

THE OTHER OFFICER *told you Amir is gay? How is that relevant? We were simply arguing about . . . oh,* something. *Something else. A complete misunderstanding. It is complicated. But I don't appreciate you saying things like that about my family.*

Nine Days Ago

VALERIO HAD PROMISED to take me on another "epic date." We were texting one morning, and he decided we would see the Sistine Chapel, because it was one of his favorite places in Rome, and apparently Goethe had written, "Until you have seen the Sistine Chapel, you can have no adequate conception of what man is capable of accomplishing."

"Never heard of this Goethe dude," I replied, making a mental note to look him up on Wikipedia later. "But that does sound pretty epic."

Now I was standing in the grand foyer of the Vatican. The ceilings were curved, high, made of fine marble. Frescoes everywhere. I was at the center of the Catholic universe. As I waited for Valerio to buy our tickets, I realized that every little thing I had done that morning felt significant. It was like a Lonely Island song.

I took a step—AT THE VATICAN.

I drank some water—AT THE VATICAN.

I took a shit—AT THE VATICAN.

That last one might have actually been significant. It was technically the holiest shit of my life.

Valerio returned with our tickets. He was looking amazing that day, wearing a tucked-in polo with jeans rolled just above the ankle. He smiled at me with those soft lips. I mean, who gave him the right?

I suppose God.

Right.

A woman with rectangular glasses and dark red lipstick directed us outside, to a large terrace where tour groups and families seemed to be getting their start. The area had massive sculptures, which the guides were describing in animated detail.

It was the hottest day since I had arrived in Rome. The sun was relentless. I decided to rest back against a ledge as Valerio took in the sculptures.

He leaned next to me. "Tired already?"

I smiled. Ledges seemed to be our thing. Valerio then nudged my waist and leaned deeper into my side.

"Is this okay?" I whispered, looking around.

Valerio pulled me in. "Do not let people tell you how to live your life, Amir."

"I just feel self-conscious, that's all."

"It is all about how you present yourself," Valerio said, smiling at a man wearing a fanny pack who was glaring at us. "If I was standing in front of the Pope and I said, 'Oh, I am *so* sorry, Mr. Pope, I am gay,' then of course he would be like, 'Yeah, no. Not cool.' But if I said, 'Hey, I am gay,' like it is my eye color, then the Pope would probably shrug and be like, 'Okay, live your truth.'" Valerio jumped off the ledge and took a bow before me. "It is all about delivery."

I smiled. "Have you always been like this?"

"Like what?"

"Confident in yourself," I said. "In talking to others. In putting yourself out there, in a place where, you know, *yourself* isn't exactly welcome."

Valerio waved his hand. "It is not confidence. It is more like— what is the word in English? *Ti costringi*. You force it." He scratched his head. "How do you say . . ."

"Fake it till you make it?" I offered.

"Yes. That."

Signs kept pointing to the Sistine Chapel, but it was nowhere in sight. There was always another glittering exhibit. Another statue. A courtyard. A bathtub. We hit a breezy courtyard, with the jankiest fountain at the center. It was almost laughable. It was just a shrub with a tiny spurt of water coming out on top. I figured it had to be a significant shrub—some chunk of holy land—but I kind of preferred not knowing.

I noticed there were pennies in the fountain, so I tossed one in. Valerio popped up next to me.

"So, where's the Sistine Chapel?" I asked.

"Is that the whole reason you are here? At the center of Catholicism, one of the most influential religions in the history of mankind?"

I pointed at Bulbasaur the Shrub. "You're calling that influential?"

Valerio sighed. "Americans."

We moved over to a statue of a strong body with curly hair, twisted in the most intricate, impossible body contortions. A snake wrapped between that statue and other figures, their elbows and arms, linking them all together.

Valerio explained the history of the sculpture—it was by three sculptors of Rhodes, it depicted a famous Trojan priest and his three sons being attacked by serpents, it was very famous—and I listened. I made sure to nod, but not too much. I wondered where Valerio was going with this. All of this. I wondered what exactly he was looking for, because even if some part of me was still traumatized from Jackson, how that had ended, I couldn't deny that Valerio and I had chemistry. We were on a second date. Something was setting in, like the moment paint starts to dry.

We moved on to the next exhibit, a hall of marble busts lined up around the circular room. I moved down the line, inspecting their faces. They all looked so calm, so at peace. It was as if the marble busts were saying, "Don't worry, Amir. Everything will be fine."

Easy for you to say, bust of Caesar. You didn't worry and look where that got you. Stabbed by Brutus.

Valerio whispered in my ear, "We should totally just *stab* Caesar."

My heart fluttered. "You've seen *Mean Girls*?"

He looked at me with a confused expression. "Of course. It is a classic. I am from Puglia, Amir; I did not grow up under a rock."

I smiled.

"So you're telling me they have movies in Puglia."

"Oh, we had more than movies. We had scenes *from* the movies. The most beautiful coast in the world." We exited the room of busts and followed another sign for Cappella Sistina, up a marble staircase. "It is still my favorite place. When I was younger, I would go and take a bag of plums—they were my favorite fruit—and sit and watch the ocean. Even when I was a teenager, I would leave my phone at home. I would go and think about life, how one day I would leave Italy."

"I don't understand why anyone would ever leave Italy," I said.

Valerio looked at me and laughed. "Of course you do not. You are American. But for us, it is different. All my mother ever wanted was for me to leave Puglia and go somewhere like London, Copenhagen, New York. But now I do not think it is possible."

"Why not?"

Valerio's jaw tensed.

"Do you remember at Rigatteria, when you looked up my university on your phone," he said, "and read that it was one of the best in Italy?"

I nodded.

"I got into a better university in England. One of the best ones in the world. But then my mother got sick. Ovarian cancer, a long, drawn-out bastard. That is why I am working so much this summer."

"Because the hospital bills are so bad?"

"What? No." Valerio looked at me like I was crazy. "Unlike in your country, we believe health care is a right. I am working because my mother cannot work in this condition. She wanted me to go to London, but with our finances, it would have been impossible. I have younger sisters in school, and there are bills to pay. I had to stay."

We approached a large door, entering what seemed like another courtyard flooded with sunlight.

"I'm sorry," I said.

"Do not be," Valerio said. We had entered an outdoor pathway connecting two chambers. No courtyard in sight. "In Italy, family is everything. It was my choice. Though maybe if I had gone to London, I would not have had cute boys falling asleep on me after a nice date."

I grinned like a fool. "How many times do I have to say it? *Italian. Food.* It's just not suitable for dates. I don't see how the words 'romantic' and 'Italian dinner' can ever be used together."

Valerio and I moved slowly across the walkway, soaking up that first moment of sunlight since we started our Vatican tour.

"What about your family?" Valerio asked.

I took a sharp breath. "I don't really talk to them anymore," I said shyly. "They're not cool with the gay thing. So I guess they're not cool with me."

Valerio grew silent. I looked over to read his expression when his eyes lit up. Suddenly, he glanced quickly over his shoulder, grabbed my arm, and tugged me forward.

He pulled me behind a wooden door that was propped open

at the end of the walkway, just before the next exhibit, into a little hiding spot in the corner. It was dark. I could hear the chatter of people, footsteps, behind the door. I opened my mouth to ask what the hell he was doing when Valerio leaned in and kissed me.

I pulled back.

"What are you doing?" I said, my eyes big and scared.

Valerio held my face and whispered, "I am cool with the gay thing. Fuck everyone else."

"But we're at the *Vatican*."

"So what?"

"So, like, Catholicism." I remembered how Jackson wore a silver cross around his neck that, when we were lying in his car with the seats reclined, would press into my arms and leave a mark. Sometimes I'd get anxious that that mark would give me away if my mom or dad ever noticed it.

I checked over my shoulder. Wall. Door. Darkness. I looked at Valerio. Cute boy. Soft, full lips. Lips that were their own art form. That deserved an entire exhibit. This whole thing was crazy, I realized, but why should a place dictate where we can and can't be ourselves? So I kissed him. Deliberately. No shame.

Even if it turned out I would never see the Sistine Chapel, I would have experienced that kiss, and it felt just as important as all these statues and painted ceilings.

Just as suddenly, Valerio pulled back and swooped around the door, tugging me with him into the next exhibit. "You tease," I said, my heart racing. Another part of me throbbing.

We were walking like fools. "You and this whole museum."

We approached a golden door at the end of the hall. *This has to be it*, I thought to myself. *This has to be the Sistine Chapel.*

Bamboozled again. It was a darker, more crowded hall with tapestries on the wall. No one was stopping to appreciate the intricate maps of the old world sewn into these cloths; we were all just shuffling through, rushing to the main event. I felt kind of bad that all these exhibits weren't getting any love.

"This must be what it feels like to open for Beyoncé," I said.

"Worse," Valerio said. "It is like if Beyoncé were opening for God."

Somehow, there was another long hall, this one with an even more spectacularly painted ceiling. But not spectacular enough, because it still wasn't the Sistine Chapel. The Catholic Church was doing the most here.

"This place needs a fast pass," I grumbled.

"It will all be worth it," Valerio reassured. "Remember what Goethe said?"

"Yeah, well, Goethe skipped a lot of steps."

Valerio shook his head. "You impatient Americans."

We sped through multiple chambers dedicated to Raphael, a contemporary art museum, the Hall of Animals. I imagined the marble zebras and lions coming to life, like the National Zoo gone wild. Maybe I was hallucinating; I hadn't had any water in hours.

Then I saw it. A big red sign at the top of a nondescript staircase: CAPPELLA SISTINA. This one was different from all the others. This one was real.

"Valerio," I whispered.

Slowly, we shuffled toward the sign, and as we passed through the door, I was expecting some kind of earth-shifting change. After all that buildup, I was expecting fireworks, laser beams, an entire spectacle.

It was a dark, cool room. It was crowded.

Valerio nudged me. "Look up."

The first thing I saw was the iconic Michelangelo image: God and Adam, heavenly homies, with their hands reaching out, fingers barely touching.

"Holy shit," I said.

"Holy shit, indeed," Valerio said.

My eyes pinged everywhere. These people, these painted figures, pale-skinned and bare and robed, holy, human, a collective fantasy, another world. High above. It all came to life before my eyes.

It was the biggest party in the world.

It was the most important room in the world.

"Hey," Valerio said. "What do you think?"

My gaze swept around the room, all the layers, the levels of this world that Michelangelo created. "Like I finally have an adequate conception of what man is capable of accomplishing," I said with a smile.

Gazing up at Michelangelo's masterpiece, I thought to myself: *I wish I could talk to Amir from a month ago. The one who thought his life was over. I wish I could have told myself it was all going to be okay. Like, hey, Past Amir. Hey, buddy. You're going to be fine. You're going to make*

great friends in Rome, and you'll sneak kisses with cute Italian boys in
the Vatican, and everything will be okay.

Valerio brushed his hand against mine, and for a few seconds, our pinkies linked. I looked up and took in the intricate design of the ceilings, the cool air of the room. I took one more look at the central image. Man and God. Adam, with his knee propped up, leaning back and leaning in at the same time.

Valerio nudged my arm. "Pretty epic, right?"

"Pretty epic," I said.

Interrogation Room 37

Amir

I DIDN'T MEAN to get into the specifics of my date with Valerio, but judging from your intense level of attention, you seemed to be okay with it. There's something about you, Officer. It's like you have a soft side.

Unfortunately, this story is about to sour like a poorly made batch of limoncello. Limoncello? It's a lemon digestif they make in Naples—digestif, it's like an aperitif. Um. Wow, and I thought I was the teenager.

Do you watch RuPaul's Drag Race, sir? You've heard of it? You say you accidentally walked into a viewing party at a sports bar thinking it was a football game? I ask because it can get dramatic, in a way only the gays can, so buckle up.

Viewer discretion is advised.

Interrogation Room 38

Soraya

HALF OF ME *wanted Amir to stay in Rome, to stay happy and live his life there. I thought I could just ignore what I had discovered. But the other half of me wanted my brother back in my life. I don't get it. I don't even like Amir that much. I'm pretty sure I like him a normal amount, for a little sister. I just wanted him back.*

Anyway, I was busy with Cats rehearsal—we had finally gotten to my part of the script—so that got in the way, too. I can't pretend it was just my internal debate. I'm not that good of a person. I was knee-deep in "Memory." It had to be perfect. I had to hit a high C. I don't know if you know music, but it's very hard.

I remember one night, I heard my parents talking in the kitchen. They didn't know I was home; I think they thought I was at rehearsal. But I had that night off. I remember my mom asking, "Well, what? Would we rather have our son be gay, or would we rather not have him at all?" And I remember my dad was just silent.

Eight Days Ago

THE MORNING AFTER my date with Valerio, I had coffee with Jahan. We met at a café on the main Viale. There was one right underneath Jahan's apartment, a narrow coffee bar where you stood and ordered—*posso avere un caffè, per favore*—but Jahan preferred the one on the Viale because it was owned by a butch lesbian Italian woman. Support your local queers, he liked to say.

"So you're in love," he said.

"With the Sistine Chapel, yes. She was beautiful. Even if she did play hard to get."

Jahan knocked back his coffee in one shot. Espresso. The Italians only drink espresso. "*Ahh.* All right, lover boy. So you're seeing him today."

"I need to work today," I said. I had promised two different people I would make their Wikipedia pages today. That was a whole month's rent.

"This weekend?"

"He's out of town. Visiting his family in Puglia."

"Oh, he's from Puglia! Poor boy. It's even hotter down there than it is here." Jahan wiped a rivulet of sweat from his forehead. Even standing at the bar directly in front of a spinning fan, we were drowning in our own sweat. "Well, you know what I say about boys."

"I don't think you've ever told me what you say about boys."

"Fuck 'em."

"Jahan."

"Yes, fuck 'em," said the café owner. She was a short-haired, short-bodied, thick-armed Italian woman with a big mole on her lip.

"See, even the lesbian said to fuck 'em!"

"I don't think she meant it the way you mean it . . ." I laughed. "Oh, Jahan. I can't believe you're leaving Rome next week."

"If I manage to pass this algebra class," Jahan said, knocking back another shot of espresso. "*Ahh*. It's not looking so good right now. I keep failing these damn practice tests. I came up, like, two questions short on the last one."

"Shut up. What the hell are we doing here, then?"

We went back to Jahan's apartment, where I practically shoved his algebra textbook into his hands. It seemed counterproductive—I wanted Jahan to stay in Rome, didn't I?—but I wanted him to pass this exam more, and I felt personally invested in it, so I quizzed him on the Pythagorean theorem and made him tell me what PEMDAS stood for, and then I made him use it to solve an annoyingly complex equation, and finally, when he was tired of my "authoritarian drill-sergeant bullshit," I forced him to take a practice test.

After he handed me his test to grade, Jahan went into his room to take a nap. I finished grading pretty quickly. He didn't do very well, so instead of waking him up, I went and flipped through some of the books scattered around his living room. There were more poetry books—poets I had never heard of, like Gwendolyn Brooks and Ocean Vuong—as well as Persian short story collections, fairy tales, the complete works of Hafiz.

After a while, Jahan emerged from his room and sat on the floor next to me.

"You should take that one," he said. I was reading the back cover of *The Pomegranate Lady and Her Sons* by Goli Taraghi. "There's a story about a polite thief who barges into this family's house in Tehran and asks if he can take their things."

"Only in Iran would the thieves have manners," I said.

"Yeah. The grandma comes out with a rifle or some shit, and the thief is just like, ma'am, please don't get violent, I'm simply going to take this expensive bowl and leave." Jahan yawned and wiped his watery eyes. "Shit gets real. Post-revolutionary Iran, man."

I shook my head. "Hey, you have some *ghey* in your eye."

"Some what?"

"*Ghey*," I repeated. "You have *ghey* in your eye."

Jahan frowned. "Amir, you're being extremely homophobic right now. . . ."

My ears got red. "No, I just . . ." I ran into the kitchen to get a paper towel, came back, and wiped the thin mucus out of Jahan's eye.

"Ohhh, you mean sleep?" Jahan said.

"Yeah, that. I can never remember the English word for it. My mom always called it '*ghey*.'"

Jahan took out his phone to look up the word on his Persian dictionary app. "So it says here that '*ghey*' means 'vomit.' Must be like vomit of the eye or something. Isn't that neat? See, I would much rather be learning Farsi than this algebra crap."

"I thought you spoke Farsi."

"I took a semester in college, but I didn't speak it growing up like you. My dad barely spoke it himself. He was second generation." Jahan patted my face. "But hey, you're as Persian as they come. And you have a little *ghey*, too."

I touched the inside of my eye, but there was nothing there. "Ahh." I rolled my eyes. "I guess I do."

The next night, Giovanni invited me over to his apartment by the Colosseum for a drink and pizza. I said sure. I thought it was important that I start hanging out more with Giovanni and his friends. Not only was Jahan leaving next week, but Neil had just told me that he and Francesco were thinking of moving to the countryside.

It wasn't like I was going home anytime soon. It had been a week since the last time my family had tried contacting me. I'd even checked my old phone that morning to see if I had any texts or voicemails from them. Nothing. As much as I wanted to believe I had moved on, I hadn't. It was like I'd torn up a letter and tossed it in the wind just to have the pieces blow back in my face.

But maybe I had to accept that this was my life now. Maybe Rome was my new home. I was even starting to think about enrolling at John Cabot, an American university in Rome. That way I could apply for a student visa. Plus, Jahan said he knew someone who worked there who could help me get a scholarship.

I decided to walk to Giovanni's instead of taking the tram. It was a trek across the river, past the ancient ruins with all the cats hanging around. The walk took nearly an hour, but I thought it might take a load off my mind.

When I got to his apartment, Giovanni opened the door in his towel. I was stunned; there were just so many abs. I didn't know a person could be in possession of that many abdominal muscles.

"Sorry," Giovanni said, slightly out of breath. "I just returned from the gym and have to take a quick shower."

"Where are the others?" I asked.

"Jahan is studying for algebra," Giovanni said, leading me through his ornate living room. "His exam is on Wednesday, but he says he will join us later. Rocco is held up at work. Here, let me fix you a drink. What do you want?"

"Whatever's easy," I said.

Giovanni poured me a drink, and we kept walking through his massive apartment, the dining room with the giant Caravaggio, all the way until we reached his changing room. It was about the size of a classroom.

"I will be quick," he said, and he went into the shower.

I gulped my first drink down fast—it was nice and cool, and

there was no air-conditioning in this beautiful apartment. When Giovanni got out of the shower, he fixed two more, one for me and one for himself. We took them back into the changing room.

"I was thinking about our conversation the other night," Giovanni said. He was standing in front of a full-length mirror, his hair dripping wet. "The Italian men, running down the street, tipping one another's hats off. Chasing one another into the darkness. I think that would make a great opening for my book."

"You don't have an opening yet?"

"I have toyed around with about ten million different ideas, but none of them seem to work," he said.

I took a big gulp of my drink. "I think that would be a cool opening, yeah."

Giovanni undid the white towel wrapped around his waist. I was sitting in the far corner of the changing room, where there was a staircase leading upstairs. "I simply need something more exciting," he said. "Something that will grab your attention."

I stared at his back. It was like a map; uncharted territory. If Jackson and Valerio were boys, the maps I knew well, then Giovanni was Westeros. His ass was in full view, and although he was covering his dick with his hand, his abs were still very much on display through the mirror.

My eyes jumped between Giovanni's body in front of me, hot, the empty glass of ice cubes in my hand, cold, and the flesh in my pants, hard.

"When do you think you'll finish your book?" I asked, my mouth dry.

"Oh, who can say?" Giovanni said. He slipped on a pair of underwear, finally. "Is a book ever really finished?"

I looked up; Giovanni was eyeing me like a wolf.

He took a step forward.

"I always thought you were handsome, Amir," Giovanni said. "From that very first party, when Jahan brought you here."

He moved closer. His abs were at eye level. "Thanks" was all I could manage to get out.

Giovanni was suddenly towering over me, one bare leg jutted forward, and somehow my arm brushed against it like he was tracing a vocabulary word in my notebook, like he was my tutor, like he was Jackson—

And then there were mouths. There were hands. There were torsos. And there was motion, from the changing area to the old couch in the dining room. It all happened so fast, but I can say it happened under the Caravaggio.

My phone fell out of my pocket. It must have been while Giovanni was pulling my pants off. I found it under one of the old chairs. Thankfully, the screen wasn't shattered, and I saw I had two missed calls from Jahan and a text from Valerio. My heart dropped.

I wasn't beholden to Valerio, I reminded myself. I wasn't beholden to anyone. Neither was Giovanni, who was in an open relationship. Still, I felt like I had just done something stupid, like driving with my eyes closed, even if I'd come out of it unscathed.

Giovanni finally put some clothes on, and we went out for

pizza, hardly saying much to each other as we zigzagged the busy side streets. It was a Saturday night. Rome was filling up with more and more tourists.

We sat down a table at a restaurant just off Piazza Santa Maria in Trastevere. I could hear the faintest sound of the fountain splashing in the background, the sound of children laughing, just like Jahan had told me.

Giovanni glanced up from the menu. "It is interesting to me how you Americans always seem to inspect your menus very carefully," he said, "as if they contain some kind of nuclear code."

I straightened my back. "They have so many different pizzas here. I don't know which one to pick."

"Just pick the one you want," Giovanni said.

He reached over and tapped my wrist. I gripped the edges of my menu. Earlier in the night, Giovanni's touch was all I wanted. He was much older than Valerio and Jackson, wealthier, more spectacularly built . . . but now I was nervous to be seen with him. Now that we were out in public, his touch felt illicit.

Giovanni pulled his hand back. "I hear you have been seeing Valerio," he said.

I frowned. "I'd appreciate if you could keep what just happened between us," I said, lowering my voice.

"Of course. But it is not like you are married," Giovanni said with a flick of his wrist.

"True." I exhaled. "How does it work with you and Rocco?"

Giovanni cocked his head. "We are not married either . . ."

"I mean the open relationship."

He let out a long sigh, the kind that dropped and hit every note in the scale. "It does not. That is how it works. Things like this happen and I do not tell him."

We ordered a pizza with cherry tomatoes and mushrooms on it, and some beer. "Are you happy with Rocco?" I asked Giovanni.

Giovanni chewed on the thought for a second. "We were happy for a while," he said. "We have been together for two years now, and I would say for the first year, we were happy ninety-five percent of the time. The next six months, seventy-five. The last six months I would say it has sunk to under fifty."

The waitress dropped off our beers. *"Salute,"* we said, clinking glasses.

"We just get into these explosive fights," Giovanni continued. "Look. I get it. I have been working on my novel for nearly five years now. I am lazy, but who isn't? I come from money, I am entitled, I attempted to be part of the family business but left to go to pilot school, then I went to college in the UK, and then I dropped out to party for a year and re-enrolled. I have lived a whole life in my twenties and it is not even over yet. But Rocco. He remains in Rome his whole life. He has been comfortable. He thinks his art is his escape, but it is not going anywhere. I keep telling him if he would just go out and see the world, his art would soar. That is all I want for him. To succeed. I believe that is the real source of our fights. It is not because I am lazy, or slutty, or all the other things he accuses me of. It is his own failure."

"Wow. The floodgates have come down," I said, genuinely shocked that Giovanni would share so much with me.

Giovanni shrugged. "I cannot talk to anyone else about it." He lit a cigarette and took a long drag, blowing the smoke across the table.

"You haven't talked to Jahan or Neil about it?"

"God, no. Jahan is very close with Rocco, and besides, you know Jahan—he can cut someone out of this group just as quickly as he can bring them in," Giovanni said. "Neil and I do not talk much, but I am sure he and Rocco hooked up at some point. He has a slutty history but wants to pretend he is a 'good girl' now."

"Really?"

"Oh yes. Don't let the domestic image fool you. Neil used to have more fun than all of us. He was a real troublemaker."

I couldn't pinpoint exactly why that made me feel sad, to think of Neil as anything but the committed boyfriend I knew him to be.

"What do you mean, Jahan can cut someone out?" I asked. "Has he done that before?"

Giovanni laughed. "Remember Gaetano?" I nodded; he was the one who read the story in Italian about how Jahan made him feel accepted. "Oh, that whole performance was bullshit. Jahan cannot stand Gaetano. He was part of our friend group for a while, but he got on Jahan's nerves, and they had some kind of beef. Snip. We stopped seeing him."

He continued: "And Gaetano—let me tell you, I do not feel bad for him one bit. He is cheating on his boyfriend, Pier Paolo. Yes, they started dating only six months ago, and Gaetano is already sleeping with Rocco. I think they are in love or something. Rocco never told me, of course. But I saw his texts with Gaetano, telling him to break up with Pier Paolo." Giovanni shook his head. "I do not even care at this point."

The waiter arrived carrying our pizza. She set it on the table, and I dove in. It burnt my tongue, the roof of my mouth, but it was delicious. And it took my mind off the fact that Giovanni had just wiped away the perfect image I had of these people, wiped it away clean like an Etch A Sketch.

"We are all pretty fucked, Amir," Giovanni added quietly, washing down the last of his beer. "I know things are not great with your family back home, but we are all quite fucked over here, too."

When we got back to Giovanni's place, Jahan opened the door for us, a glass of wine in hand.

"You're back!" he exclaimed. "Finally. Rocco's gone and raided the liquor cabinet. He's in a bit of a grumpy mood. How was dinner?"

"Dinner was good," Giovanni said. "We went to that pizza place off Piazza Santa Maria."

"That's the one with the owner who used to own the kebob shop on the Viale, no?" Jahan said. "Remember when the Bengali worker got locked in that basement and everyone thought it was the owner who did it? They must have had major beef. Or should I say, shawarma . . ." Jahan snickered to himself. "Anyway, Rocco is guzzling whiskey or scotch, something manly like that, in the living room. I'm a classy lady, so I'm sticking to wine."

Giovanni went and poured himself a glass of wine. He asked if I wanted one, and I said I was good.

"You have been working very hard lately, Jahan," Giovanni said.

"Don't remind me. I'm actually stressed," Jahan moaned. "I shouldn't even be here right now."

"You'll be fine," I said to him. "You were a beast with the Pythagorean theorem yesterday. You're going to kill it."

Jahan nodded. "Yeah, I hope so."

We gathered around the dining room, under the Caravaggio. I quickly scanned the room for any trace of Giovanni and me. A hair, a sock, anything we might have left behind when we were hooking up.

"Caravaggio never had to learn algebra," Jahan muttered.

"Caravaggio murdered someone, did he not?" Rocco said. He was sitting on the couch where Giovanni and I had gotten frisky just a couple hours earlier.

Giovanni rolled his eyes. "Yes, and it got him exiled from Rome. Which is one way to get someone out of this city."

Rocco glared at his boyfriend and said something sharp in Italian.

"I suppose da Vinci was a mathematical genius," Jahan said, defusing the tension. "So maybe there's some merit to knowing math as an artist."

"Plus, he had all those hidden clues in his artwork," I added.

"Ooh, someone's seen *The Da Vinci Code!*" Jahan teased. I blushed. That was definitely how I knew that.

We finished our drinks and moved on to the bar, some kind

of basement spot where I got carded for the first time in Italy. Giovanni and Rocco were bickering on and off, and within five minutes they had to go back outside for a full-on argument. Jahan and I turned our attention to one of the many screens in the bar; they were all playing dramatic scenes from decades' worth of gay movies. Jahan was shocked that I had hardly seen any of them, and he made me pull out my phone and take down the names: *God's Own Country, Milk, Paris Is Burning*. It was a long list.

"What's going on with Giovanni and Rocco?" I asked.

"Oh, they're always like this," Jahan said. "I'm surprised you haven't noticed before."

I inhaled sharply. The air was smoky down there. "How close are you with Rocco?"

Jahan smiled. "Rocco is my best friend in the world."

"What about Gaetano?"

Jahan turned. "What about him?"

"I, I just—" I stammered. "He told that story the other night."

"He sure did," Jahan said, rolling his eyes. "No, Gaetano's fine. He's sweet. We're just not that close anymore."

I couldn't help but see Jahan in a different light after what Giovanni had told me. He wasn't just the sun of the friend group; Jahan was also the shade, capable of shutting people out of his sunlight.

Somehow, despite Rocco and Giovanni's fighting, we stayed out until six in the morning. At the end of the night, we all walked back to their apartment by the Colosseum and hugged goodbye. Before he turned around with Rocco, Giovanni winked at me. Jahan definitely noticed, but I didn't say anything.

Jahan walked back with me across the glistening Tiber River. It was six thirty by the time I got home. I had a snack—leftover bread sticks—and passed out with crumbs all over my bed. When I woke up, I thought I was still dreaming, because someone had commented on my last Instagram post.

"Thx for fucking my fucking boyfriend"

Six Days Ago

IT WAS NINE thirty, almost ten in the morning. I deleted the comment right away and texted Giovanni, but he wasn't responding. Then I texted Jahan. Miraculously, he was awake, so I put on some clothes and ran over to his apartment, arriving sweaty and out of breath.

"Well, you did the impossible," Jahan said. He slammed the door shut. "You got me up in the morning."

His apartment was significantly messier than it was just a few days ago. There were sheets of graph paper everywhere, a TI-83 calculator atop a stack of books, a textbook on the armchair. Jahan pushed the textbook off the chair and sat down.

"You won't believe what Rocco did," I said.

"What *Rocco* did? Honey, I already talked to Rocco and Giovanni. Why didn't you tell me what happened last night?"

"Oh. I don't know," I said, pacing in front of him. "I guess I just didn't think it was a big deal. We didn't actually . . . God. How did

Rocco find out anyway? Was it the wink at the end of the night? Did he find a hair on the couch or something?"

"Really? That's what you're worried about?"

"And I can't believe he would comment on my Instagram! I asked you all not to follow or tag me there, because I didn't want . . ." I cut myself off. "I guess I never asked Rocco specifically, but Jesus."

Jahan looked at me like I was going mad.

"I thought they were open," I mumbled.

"Amir. They broke up."

My jaw fell. "What?"

"Giovanni called me," Jahan said, rubbing his eyes. "He was frantic. He told me Rocco found out about the two of you, and then something else came up, and they both started yelling at each other and throwing things, and Rocco just broke up with him."

I stared at a poster of the ruins of Pompeii, right above where Jahan was sitting. "This is all my fault," I said.

Jahan looked at me and sighed. "You need to be more careful, Amir. You've gotten yourself in the middle of something you don't understand."

My head was processing the words Jahan was saying, but my heart seemed to have short-circuited.

I felt absolutely terrible. Like I had let Jahan down. He was tired, and serious, in a way I had never seen in him before—there wasn't an ounce of his usual lightness.

Jahan picked up the algebra book and held it on his lap. "*Cazzo.*

I really didn't need this right now," he said under his breath.

We were quiet for a second, until the sound of my phone buzzing broke the silence. Jahan raised his eyebrows.

"Who's calling?" he asked.

"God, I hope it isn't Rocco," I said, reaching into my pocket. I looked at the caller ID on the screen—*Roya Azadi;* she was calling on Facebook Messenger—and shoved it back in.

"Anyway, I'm really sorry," I said quickly, "for causing drama with your friends, right before your algebra exam, but I'm sure you'll—" My phone buzzed again.

"Who keeps calling you?" Jahan said, getting up from his chair.

"No one, don't worry."

"Is it Rocco? Giovanni?"

I took my phone out to silence it. "No, it's—"

Jahan grabbed my hand, twisted it, and looked at my screen. "Who is Roya Azadi?" he asked.

My heart started racing.

"It's my mom."

Jahan gasped. "Amir! You should answer it!"

"No, I shouldn't." I felt dizzy.

"I understand it's an awkward time, but maybe your family is sorry," Jahan said. "Maybe they want to apologize."

"Jahan, trust me," I insisted. "It's not important right now."

"Oh, forget this other stuff," Jahan said, swatting his hand. "This is family. It's important. How can they just *reject* you like that? We're Iranian. Family comes first. Sure, our parents immigrated over with certain values, but they immigrated over for you to be *happy*, first and foremost. You need to talk to them. It could be . . ."

I collapsed onto the chair Jahan had been sitting on moments ago. Now I was the one rubbing my eyes, cupping my face in my hands. My heart was going haywire. I felt everything crumbling.

"Amir, are you okay?" Jahan placed a hand on the side of my arm. Then I felt something shift in him, like a twitch. "You know, I never asked you what your parents said when you came out to them, but if it was bad . . ."

I shook my head, once.

"It was *that* bad? Fucking assholes."

I kept shaking my head. My whole body was quivering. "It's not that. It's not that," I said. The weight of the lie was crushing my heart. "They're not bad people," I said, hoping that would relieve some of the pain.

"Not bad people?" Jahan spat. "They kicked you out. That's the definition of 'bad people.'"

"It's not like that."

"Then what was it like? Did they give two weeks' notice? A nice severance package? Was it a light tap out the door?"

"Jahan. I'm just saying it was *like* they kicked me out."

"Either they kicked you out or they didn't!" Jahan's voice was an angry mob, a million street signs pointing in different directions. But then it turned kind. That really killed me. "Shit. I'm sorry. I didn't mean to pry. You know, when you first told us about your family, Neil and I both agreed we didn't want to trigger you, we didn't want to push you to talk about any of this before you were ready. Here, we'll talk about it later. Lord knows we're both tired, and there's enough—"

"I never came out to my parents," I blurted. "I'm sorry. I just never came out to them. I never got to."

Interrogation Room 37

Amir

I STILL CAN'T *stop picturing Jahan's face when I told him the truth, that I hadn't been kicked out. The way he looked at me, with total disappointment written all over his face.*

I still can't stop looping through our conversation.

Six Days Ago

"SORRY, I'M JUST trying to understand what's going on," Jahan finally said. "You never came out to them? So when you told us they kicked you out . . ."

"It was a lie." I had to practically pry the words from my mouth. "It's hard to explain. I—I never really had the chance to come out to my parents. A kid at my school saw me kissing another boy, and he took a picture of it, and he was going to show it to my parents unless I paid him a bunch of money, so I left."

"What the fuck? Amir." Jahan moved closer to me on the armchair, pulled me in for a side-hug. "Buddy. I'm sorry. That sucks to an extreme degree. Why didn't you report him to the police?"

"That never really crossed my mind," I said.

"That kid should be locked up. There have to be laws about blackmail; you could have scared the shit out of him."

"Maybe."

"Anyway, that's insane," Jahan said. "Absolutely insane. But seriously, why didn't you just *tell* us that?"

"I don't know," I said. "I guess I didn't want you guys to assume anything. I didn't want to have to explain. I thought you would have all these questions, or think I just left my family and didn't give them a chance. But I knew. I knew they wouldn't . . . Anyway, that's why Rome has been so amazing. When I got here, I was sad because I felt like my real family had already rejected me, but then you guys swooped in and *became* my family. It was so surreal. All those times we were drinking prosecco in the park together, I wanted to pinch myself. Or when you and your friends would be belting those old singers you love, it was like *American* fucking *Idol*. I didn't want to ruin that. I didn't want it all to go away."

Jahan said nothing. His lips were pressed into a tight half smile.

"My whole life, I've felt like I was fighting this losing battle at home, with who I was." I fumbled for the right words. "I was keeping a scoreboard—it's hard to explain, but the points were never in my favor. They just weren't. Then I came to Rome, and the points started adding up, you know? They were finally in my favor, and I felt like I was winning."

"That's sweet, Amir. It really is," Jahan finally said. "But maybe now you can give your family a chance? At the very least, it seems like they want to talk to you."

"Maybe," I said with a sigh.

But Jahan wasn't done. "I just wish you hadn't lied to us," he continued. "That's all. You can't be doing this shit, buddy. We all believed this really bad thing had happened to you, and—"

"A really bad thing *did* happen to me."

"Well, yeah, of course. But you know what I mean. It sucks

what happened, but it also sucks that you didn't feel you could be honest about it with us."

I didn't want to be angry at Jahan. I really didn't. But something in me needed more than just "it sucks" from him.

"Well. I'm sorry I lied," I muttered.

Jahan gave me a look. "Hey, no need to roll your eyes. I'm just saying, I wish you had trusted us. I'm not angry at you. It's just, on top of this Giovanni thing, well . . . none of this is ideal, let me tell you that. None of this."

"Yeah, well, what happened to me back home wasn't ideal, either."

"Oh, come on, Amir. Don't make me out to be the asshole here."

"I'm not calling you an asshole!" I realized, too late, that I was shouting now.

Jahan opened his mouth to say something but stopped. "Amir, you're giving me a real headache right now. This is the last thing I need. First you hook up with Giovanni and his relationship blows up, and then you lie to us—"

"So it's about Giovanni, then," I said, cutting him off. "The real reason you're angry is that I broke up Giovanni and Rocco."

"I'm not happy about that, that's true."

I fought down the giant lump in my throat.

"I'm sorry I've become such a burden to you and your friends," I said softly.

"A burden? Jesus! Where is this coming from?" Jahan massaged his forehead with one hand. "I'm just saying you fucked up a bit, that's all. You hooked up with a guy you would have been wise *not* to hook up with—and if you'd asked me, I could have told you that. On top of that, you lied to us about what's going on with your family—which, again, if you had told me—"

"I'm telling you now!"

"Yeah, great timing, Amir," Jahan said, massaging his forehead with both hands now. "Look, can we talk about this later? My head is pounding, and I need to get back to studying."

I could feel my lips quivering. I wanted to tell Jahan the whole story—the specifics of Jackson and Jake, the phone calls with my parents that had played out exactly how I'd expected—but then I saw him glance nervously at his algebra textbook on the coffee table. I realized that I didn't want to do any more damage than I had already done.

So I left.

Four Days Ago

ONE OF MY favorite things about Jackson was that he made amazing playlists. He had one called "sad bops" that I especially loved. He called them sad bops because they were moody, but not necessarily depressing.

"That's the difference between sad songs and sad bops," Jackson had told me once, while we were listening to the playlist in his car. His seat was leaned back, and I was resting my head in the dimple of his chest. "Sad songs are for when your heart is broken."

"So when do you listen to sad bops?" I asked.

He shrugged. "When your heart is confused, I guess."

Now, several months later, when my own heart didn't know how it should feel, I must have looped through that playlist about eight hundred times since my fight with Jahan. I could tell you exactly which song came next. After "Dancing On My Own" by Robyn, it was "Supercut" by Lorde. "Wrecking Ball" by Miley Cyrus. "Light On" by Maggie Rogers.

I spent all that time holed up in my apartment, eating fried risotto balls from the pizza shop downstairs for every meal. The greasy paper bags were starting to pile up on my kitchen counter.

My brain was looping through its own confused playlist: Was Jahan mad at me? Why hadn't Giovanni responded to my text asking if he was okay? And what about Rocco? He had made it very clear that he hated me now. Would he hurt me? Should I call my family? And then back to Jahan—should I call him?

It felt like the ground beneath my feet was crumbling away and there was nothing I could do about it.

It was the loneliest I had felt in a long time. It reminded me of all those weekends I'd spent holed up inside my room back home, when I couldn't tell Jackson about what Ben and Jake had threatened me with, when I couldn't talk to my parents or Soraya.

Rome wasn't supposed to feel like this.

I went to Tiberino, the restaurant on the island, to try and get some work done. I was supposed to be writing a Wikipedia page for another start-up the cryptocurrency guys had referred me to, some social networking start-up—because that was just what the world needed: another website for making friends. I couldn't focus though. There were too many people around, too many tourists and happy families.

Plus, my table was wobbly. That was annoying as hell. I got a stack of napkins and crouched underneath the table to stuff them under one of the legs.

"What are you doing?"

I looked up and saw Laura's ring-studded fingers.

"Dude, why don't you just move to a different table?" she said.

"This whole outdoor area is on a slope," I muttered, coming up. "You guys should fix that."

"Never seemed to bother you before."

We kissed one another on each cheek.

"It's good to see you," I said. "I've had a shitty couple of days."

Laura looked at me funny. "Actually, I've been trying to find you," she said, pulling up a chair. "I don't know if this is going to help, but I wanted to tell you . . . your sister slid into my DMs."

"How do you even know that expression—wait, *what?*"

"I did not respond," Laura said quickly. She showed me the message on Instagram: *hey, sorry if this is random, but I saw my brother Amir created your Wikipedia page and edited some other Italian pages. Do you know where he is? Is he in Italy?*

"Oh, fuck," I said, rubbing my eyes. "Shit. Shit, shit, shit. I really don't need this right now."

"Don't need what?" Laura asked. There were other people around, so she leaned in and lowered her voice. "What's going on?"

"I'd rather not talk about it," I said.

"You're going to have to," Laura said firmly. "This is suspicious as hell. I thought maybe you had murdered someone or done something sketchy! I checked your Instagram, and I noticed you haven't posted anything from Rome. I need you to explain what's going on."

Laura was waiting for me to say something. I sat there with my hands on the table, balled up in fists. I flattened them.

"Listen, Laura. I'm gay. And my family, they're not particularly cool with that. So I'm sort of just . . . here, hiding out. That's the truth."

"Oh." And then, after a pause: "Your sister is not cool with it?"

"No, she's fine. But it's my parents," I said.

"Are they religious?" Laura asked. Jackson had asked the same question when we talked about coming out to our families.

I sighed. "Yes and no. It's more a culture thing. Our culture is pretty conservative, even if you're not religious. Like, my parents and I have never even talked about sex. I always knew that when and if I came out to them, it would be like two coming-outs: 'Mom and Dad, first of all, I'm a sexual being, and then oh yeah, and I like dudes.'"

"Wow. I'm sorry." Laura laughed, but her eyes were sympathetic. "I had no idea."

"It's okay," I said quietly.

Laura looked back at the restaurant. "I haven't told my parents, either. About me. They're not religious or anything, I just . . . I don't know. They're traditional in some ways. They think I'm like this"—she gestured at her cropped hair, her studded tank top, her Doc Martens—"because I'm an artist."

We stared at each other for a second.

"Besides," Laura continued, "I'm bi. I could still end up with a man. That sounds awful, doesn't it? Like, 'There's a chance I might not be a fucking weirdo in the eyes of my parents.'"

"No, it's not awful! I think that's a totally reasonable thing to think," I said. "It would make your life a lot easier."

"But life's not supposed to be easy, you know?"

"Sometimes I wish it were."

"It wasn't easy for old Bartholomew over there," Laura said, gesturing to the church. She made a skin-peeling gesture over her face and I just about died laughing. An old man reading a newspaper a few tables over muttered something at us in Italian, and Laura snapped right back at him.

"Damn," I said. "You're kind of a badass. You know that?"

"Of course I do."

I leaned back into my chair a little and exhaled. "So, what's Rome like for people our age? I've been hanging out with these older gay guys here, and I feel like maybe I should . . . start branching out."

"Honestly? It's kind of shit," Laura said. "I like college in America better. My girlfriend and I met at a frat party, just like in the movies. Still, Rome can be all right. You'll have to come have a drink with my friends and me sometime."

I nodded. "Yeah. I'd like that."

That evening, I met Neil at Rigatteria for our Italian lesson. It had honestly been a relief to finally hear from him; it had been a few days, and I was starting to believe maybe he was pissed off at me, too.

"We missed you this weekend," Neil said. We were sitting at

the small table in the corner where we had our first lesson.

"Come on. You know there was no way I could come," I said.

"What do you mean?"

I gave him a look. I realized Neil legitimately had no idea what had happened. I explained all the drama to him: the hookup, the breakup, Jahan finding out.

"Hey," Neil said, rubbing my shoulder. "None of that is your fault."

"I shouldn't have hooked up with Giovanni."

He shrugged. "Okay, yeah. Maybe you shouldn't have done that."

"Hey!" I elbowed him lightly, and he chuckled.

"They were a messy couple anyway," Neil said. "Bound to break up eventually. I was with Rocco a long time ago, just for a little bit, and oh man. I know what he's like. Combined with Giovanni's entitlement . . . well, it was only a matter of time."

I glanced down at the bracelets on Neil's arms—one made out of turquoise beads, the other black beads. I had asked him about them once and he said the first one was a gift from an old girl-friend, from back when he was "straight," and the second one he'd gotten with Francesco when they went to Madagascar spontane-ously for their one-year anniversary. Then I noticed the engage-ment ring on his finger.

"Remember when you told me sometimes you don't recognize that person?" I said, pointing at his ring. "Right after Francesco proposed. You were drunk, and you were like, 'sometimes I can't believe I'm, like, this serious, committed person now.' It's funny because that's the only 'you' I know. It's hard to believe you once dated Rocco."

"I guess there's more to people than meets the eye," Neil said.

"Yeah. About that." I hesitated, then I turned to him. "I didn't really tell you guys the truth about my family. They never kicked me out. I left home before I even had the chance to come out to them."

Neil's eyes grew wide. "Oh."

"It's a long story, but basically someone at my school was going to out me, so I ran."

"Ah."

"And I just didn't think . . ." I bit my lip. "I wish I had told you guys from the beginning. I wish I could go back in time to that dinner party and just suck it up and tell the truth."

"You're telling the truth now," Neil said.

I tried to smile. "I don't know what I feel worse about, that or the Giovanni thing."

"Again. Not. Your. Fault."

"It was so stupid of me, though. Giovanni had just invited me to Umbria, and I thought maybe we'd be friends and I wouldn't be alone after Jahan leaves . . ."

"Um, hello? Aren't I your friend?" Neil nudged me. "In fact, I have an idea. Come with Francesco and me to our mountain home. It won't be nearly as glamorous as Giovanni's villa in Umbria, but the view is amazing. We're driving up after Jahan's goodbye party."

I wanted to, but I didn't know if I trusted myself, after how I had messed up Giovanni and Rocco's relationship, not to do the same with Neil and Francesco. But then I thought about it: Neil was a genuine friend. And this was a genuine, friendly invite.

"*Grazie*," I said. "I'd love to."

We gave up on the Italian lesson and moved up to the rooftop. About twenty people were drinking and chatting under the fairy lights, a mixed crowd of men and women, young and old, while a band played folk music.

"So that singer I was telling you about," I said. "I was talking to her today. She said my sister messaged her on Instagram. How crazy is that?"

Neil looked surprised. "What did she say?"

"My sister wanted to know where I am." I sighed. "I miss her a lot. I really do. I was thinking, maybe if I make enough money, I could buy her a plane ticket or something to come visit me. But I don't want her knowing where I am. Not yet."

"Have you tried talking to your family? I know you said you left without coming out to them, but now that they know—"

"I can't," I said, interrupting him. "Not anymore. Trust me, I've tried."

"How do you know they won't come around?"

I sighed again. "I guess I don't. I don't know that someday they won't come around. But why should I have to disrupt my life, make it that much harder, just to get them to understand something so simple about me?"

Neil didn't say anything. My eyes wandered over to the band playing.

"You know, that singer and I are sort of friends now. Her name's Laura Pedrotti. I could ask if she wants to perform here sometime. She's really incredible—I've listened to her songs on Spotify, and she's insanely talented."

"Uh, sure," Neil said absently. "That would be great."

"Cool. I'll ask her when we get back from the mountains."

Interrogation Room 38

Roya Azadi

WE JUST WANTED our son back. It had been weeks since his disappearance. I was crying myself to sleep at night. I couldn't see anything clearly anymore; I was grasping for an explanation, for something to make sense, because what didn't make sense was that Amir was not home.

My husband and I had been calling Amir for days, but he wouldn't pick up. The last thing we wanted was for him to think we had abandoned him. We understood how the tone of our last phone calls might have made him feel. So we went and talked to Soraya.

Interrogation Room 38

Soraya

THEY CAME INTO *my room when I was practicing "Memory"*
for, like, the millionth time. I had just gotten to the key change. Touch
me! It's so easy to—Um, these walls are soundproof, right? Anyway,
they knocked on my door and asked to talk.

Talking to my parents when I knew Amir was in Rome made
my stomach hurt. Even if we had stopped talking about Amir,
I was constantly thinking about him. So for them to sit on my
bed and ask, "Soraya, do you know where your brother is?" I
just about thought I was going to blow up. My whole body was
screaming.

I told them I did know, as a matter of fact, but that I wouldn't tell
them where he was. They were not happy with this answer.

Before I spilled the beans, I made my parents promise that they
would try to understand. I made them promise that they would listen
to Amir. That no matter what, they would still love him.

And my mom went, "Of course we'll love him." She said, "We love him, and we love you, more than anything. No matter what." My dad didn't say anything.

So I told them. I showed them the Instagram post of Amir reading that poem at that bar. That's when we got in touch with Neil.

Interrogation Room 39

Afshin Azadi

I'D RATHER NOT *get into the specifics of our argument on the plane.*

Three Days Ago

I DIDN'T THINK it was good etiquette to show up at a goodbye party for someone who might hate me, but I showed up anyway. It felt wrong not to be there for Jahan's last night in Rome—even if it meant facing Giovanni and Rocco, too.

It was a surprise party. People started to trickle in, and we were waiting to hear from Jahan after his exam. I didn't even know half the people there, on the rooftop of Rigatteria. Some of them were familiar faces from Garbo, like the woman with the FEMME RAGE tattoo.

What would my life in Rome look like after Jahan left? It was a selfish thing to wonder as we took our positions hiding behind all the furniture and antique doors and mirrors for Jahan's last big night in Rome, but I wondered it anyway. I was pretty sure I had gotten a taste of it these past couple days. I pictured my life in Rome like the nipple ring in Jahan's story, dangling off a thread.

"He passed!" someone screamed. "He passed his exam! But now he's saying he's tired and doesn't want to meet us for a drink."

"Cazzo."

"Tell him to get his ass over here," Neil said.

We all got quiet while someone got on the phone with Jahan and demanded he meet them for "a drink." *"Stronza, vieni qui,"* they told Jahan over the phone. "Bitch, get over here." At least my Italian was getting better.

Eventually, Jahan agreed to come, and we all got back in our hiding positions and waited. Finally, someone whispered that he was coming up the stairs.

"Sorpresa!"

"Surprise!"

Jahan was genuinely floored; as in, he fell to the floor, laughing and crying. He was in such good spirits after passing his exam. He floated around the crowd. He hugged everyone. But when he got to me, he just smiled and gave me a quick hug. It even seemed shorter than the others, like he was barely acknowledging me.

There was a projector screen in the front of the room, rolling through old photos and videos of Jahan and his friends. Every time I looked over at this screen, it was a younger Jahan with green hair, or Jahan dancing through a museum lobby I didn't recognize, or Jahan and Rocco dressed up as Sonny and Cher for Halloween. It made me think maybe I didn't know Jahan as well as I thought I did.

My parents loved to go through old photos and videos of Soraya and me at home. I remembered just a couple of months ago, right after Ben and Jake had begun blackmailing me, we were gathered in our living room, celebrating the Persian New Year, which always falls on the first day of spring. My dad put on a video from when I was six. Soraya was a baby, and in it, I was inspecting her face, her cheeks. Then suddenly she hiccupped and cried. My parents laughed. *"Aww, jigari,"* a weird term of endearment that means "liver."

It made me wonder if we owe our parents that kind of simple, unfiltered happiness for the rest of our lives. Why couldn't they find our hiccups now as cute as they were back then? Who had changed—them or me?

Throughout the night, Jahan would stop and stare at the projector screen, too. He was lost in the nostalgia. I hardly existed to him that night. It was like this summer had never happened. We were like strangers at the bar. The party continued, and I overheard him from just a few feet away talking about how relieved he was to be done with algebra.

"It was like the one thing I've wanted most my entire life," he said, "hinged on the one thing I'm not good at."

A group of Italians stood chatting and laughing at the end of the bar, next to a broken mirror; I recognized one of them, a girl with punk-rocker hair, as a friend of Rocco's. There were two other girls next to me whispering in Italian. I found Neil and hung out with him for a while.

"Giovanni and Rocco never came," Neil said to me.

I nodded, my gaze focused on Jahan. He was waving his hands wildly and pedaling his feet. "Probably for the best," I muttered.

The people around Jahan burst into laughter.

I stayed all the way until the end of the party. Even though I lived in Testaccio, I walked back to Trastevere alongside Jahan and one of his friends, someone whose name I don't remember. It was five in the morning. They were yelling Italian curse words loudly through the streets as we crossed the bridge over the Tiber. It was a long walk, and I was mostly silent. As much as I wanted closure, I couldn't bear to bring up my problems, not on Jahan's last night here in Rome.

We said goodbye at a small intersection in Trastevere. It was unspectacular. Plain. Like saying goodbye at the end of another day. There was nothing about staying in touch, nothing about our time together in Rome and everything I had learned from him. Jahan left Rome, our Rome, much like I had left my family.

Interrogation Room 38

Roya Azadi

I DON'T MEAN to be rude, but I have to wonder why this is taking so long.

You're saying Amir won't stop talking? If you could kindly tell him that he can talk to us, I would appreciate that.

May I ask why you just laughed? No, I believe that was a laugh. I hope I am not being disrespectful, it's just I believe when I told you that Amir could talk to us, you laughed. Soraya, please. It's all right. I can handle this.

Officer, I see the way you look at me: at my clothes, my skin, my accent. You think that I wouldn't understand my son. Because of my culture, you make certain assumptions about my beliefs. And I won't lie—it was difficult, learning that Amir was gay. It has not been an easy road. For me or for my husband. But we are trying our best to understand.

I am not comfortable speaking up like this. I have not been comfortable this entire time. Many times, in this country, however, I am made to feel uncomfortable, just like this. It is normal for me, to feel that I have *walked into a party that I was not invited to. To be interrogated. To have my every value, every detail of my existence, questioned.*

Soraya, you may experience this in life, too. People will make you uncomfortable. And I do believe, firmly, that most of the time, you should not cause a scene. You should not let people get to you. But there are times when you have to defend yourself, when the things you love most dearly are thrown into question.

You look at me, ma'am, like I'm not capable of loving my own son. And that hurts. Because no matter where I come from, I am a mother before I am anything else. Ever since Soraya told us that Amir is—that he is gay, I have imagined how his life would be different, living a life like that. How much more difficult it would be. I have so many questions. I don't fully understand what he is going through. But in every single one of those scenarios, I am in my son's life. I am there for him. I will always, always be there for my Amir.

Interrogation Room 39

Afshin Azadi

Two Days Ago

THE DRIVE UP to the mountains was spectacular. Neil sat in the front with Francesco, while I kept the dogs company in the back seat. We drove through winding, twisty roads, and as we got closer to the mountains, we passed rolls of hay shaped like giant Fruit Roll-Ups. One of the dogs was nestled under the driver's seat, and the other rested her head out the window, her floppy ears swimming in the wind.

I gazed out the window next to her, thinking about how I had left things in Rome. If I even had anything to go back to there. I hadn't heard from Valerio since our Sistine Chapel date, and I was afraid to text him—he had probably heard what happened, that I'd hooked up with Giovanni and ruined his relationship. He probably wanted nothing to do with me. He'd had his heart broken before. Why risk it again?

The dog licked my face, and I smiled.

We had a picnic that afternoon in a huge field. The air was chilly. The grass was tall and weeds whipped all around us. We were surrounded by the most spectacular view of mountains and flatland, endless green fields. There was a hut out in the distance. "For the cow herders," Neil said. It was all very *Brokeback Mountain*. Francesco had prepared a basket of fresh prosciutto, bread, and different cheeses. We made little sandwiches and lay out on a picnic blanket and took in the fresh, cool air.

We took a walk around L'Aquila. It was an ancient Italian city an hour and a half north of Rome that had been ruined by an earthquake about a decade ago. Walking around was surreal. It was like the whole city was holding its breath. We walked down these shade-covered alleys, one side an old house, the walls painted yellow, half-covered in dirt, cracking, and the other side scaffolding. A new construction. But left deserted. There were abandoned mansions. There was construction and scaffolding, cranes hanging from the sky, but no one was working on it. Francesco said that the city jumped right into revitalization after the earthquake, into rebuilding itself, but they ran out of money. So all of a sudden, the development stopped. He said he was hopeful it would pick up again soon.

We had dinner at an outdoor restaurant, hidden away from civilization, in what seemed like the middle of the woods. It was the best meal of my life. The owner came out and explained, in Italian, that they had no formal staff, that the kitchen was entirely operated by family. The grandma, the *nonna*, would come out with each plate of food. There were so many plates. A meat and cheese plate with wild boar, reindeer—meats I never thought I'd get to try. A butternut squash soup that I was skeptical about sharing but now wish I could share with the entire world. And of course, the pasta. There was squid ink pasta that tasted like it had been pulled fresh out of the ocean, and eggy, yolky carbonara, and a rigatoni in tomato sauce that would have blown your mind. We finished the meal with dessert—reluctantly, since I didn't have room, but Francesco and Neil insisted—and I am so happy they did. I could have happily died with that tiramisu as my last bite of food.

Back at their mountain home, a small apartment in a complex with another family, I slept in a lofted bed. I was relieved that there was no sexual tension whatsoever—not that that giant meal would have allowed for it, as I had learned with Valerio. In fact, Francesco and Neil were very friendly. We watched a movie before going to bed: *Milk*, since Neil, like Jahan, was disappointed I hadn't seen it yet. I cried. It's discomforting, now, to think of that perfect day in the mountains. I fell asleep so full, so happy. And now I'm hungry again. Not just for food, but for the love I thought I had in Italy.

Interrogation Room 39

Afshin Azadi

THAT IS ABSURD; *I would never hurt my son. It was an argument. A disagreement. I wish we had not raised our voices like that, in public, on an airplane of all places, but that was how it happened. You can assure those passengers that their concern was not necessary; I would never lay a hand on Amir.*

Yes, of course I love my son! I love my son more than words can say. I don't like that . . . part of him that you keep mentioning, that specific part that we were arguing about on the airplane. But I love Amir.

I can see from your expression that you are confused. I will not lie; I am confused, too. I don't know, I haven't figured out how to reconcile those two feelings. I kept telling Amir we'll work on it. But what if he doesn't change?

That was the part that hurt most. He kept saying, "It's not going away. I'm not changing." Because if Amir doesn't change, then that image that I had my whole life, his future—it is all wiped away. I pictured him with a certain kind of job, a house and income and wife, a certain life. Not because I am small-minded, but because I want my son to be happy and stable. Because I know what he is capable of.

When Amir was young, we used to solve multiplication tables in the doctor's office. His mother was always worried about his health, and if he so much as coughed or sniffled, she would make me take him to the doctor. So we were there a lot, and we passed the time with math. He was brilliant, Amir. He knew every answer: six times nine, twelve times fifteen, twenty times twenty-two. He solved every problem I gave him in the snap of my fingers. I remember thinking he was going to be a doctor himself one day. Maybe a scientist like his dad. My son was going to go further than I ever had. That much I knew.

And so it is difficult, sir, to see him changing like this, so drastically. It changes the image that I had for him.

The world is a hard place, sir. It is even harder for people who are different. I know this firsthand. I don't want Amir to know that.

When I was in my twenties, I knew a boy named Michael. He and I were lab partners together in my PhD program. Michael was brilliant. I was not the most organized person back then—I did not have all my systems in place—but thanks to Michael, I passed every advanced chemistry class. We were a team. Once I asked Michael if he had a girlfriend, and he told me he did not, that he was—that he was not interested in women. I responded politely, but Michael, I believe, got the message. It was near the end of the semester, and the following semester, we chose different lab partners.

I lost touch with Michael. Last week, as I was thinking about Amir, I looked Michael up on Facebook. I found him. He is alive. He seems happy with his, um, family. I remember back to when I was a student, how disgusted I felt—betrayed, almost—by what I had learned about my lab partner. I don't know how I feel about it now, but I did send Michael a friend request. I am still waiting to see if he will accept.

I don't want to lose Amir like that. My love for Amir—the boy I raised doing multiplication tables in the doctor's office, the boy I taught how to drive, the boy I—it's too much. I can't lose him.

So to answer your question, yes. I love Amir. I am not certain about all the other things, but I am certain that I love my son.

One Day Ago

SOMEONE WAS TAPPING the side of my bed. I craned my head over the edge, my eyes still half-closed. Neil was standing below, the sun shining behind him through the sliding glass door to the apartment.

"Hey," Neil said. "Hey, Amir. Wake up."

"*Buongiorno,*" I said, opening my eyes.

Neil was looking at me in a very serious way. I heard footsteps outside, a group of people coming up the apartment building stairs.

"I don't really know how to tell you this . . ." Neil's voice trailed off.

The footsteps grew louder and louder until they reached the balcony outside the apartment. I gave Neil a confused look. Then the sliding glass door unlocked, and Francesco appeared with three people I knew very well.

It was my family.

I jumped and hid under the covers. I became a child in the dark. *If the monster can't see me, it won't find me.*

Neil tapped the floorboard underneath my bed. "Amir, I know this might come as a surprise to you—"

"No, no, no. *No!*" I yelled. "What the hell is going on, Neil? Why didn't you tell me about this?"

Neil looked at my parents nervously. "We were afraid that if I told you, you might run off again."

I could hear my mom and dad and sister breathing heavily. An infinite number of questions were swirling in my head. What was happening? How did they find me here? Were Francesco and Neil really in on this?

Some part of me wanted to go down and leap into my mom's arms, smother Soraya with kisses, but I stayed hidden under the sheets.

"Amir." My mom croaked my name. She was so close; I could see her fingertips inches from me, on the edge of the mattress. I wanted to reach out and hold her hand so badly. "Please, come down. Please. I love you, *joonam*. Come home."

"Come on, Amir," my sister pleaded.

"Come, *baba jaan*," my dad said. "Come."

I was cornered. I looked out from under the sheets, and there they were, lined up in a row: Maman, Baba, Soraya. Their eyes were tired; my mom's were even puffy and red. My chest was burning, like I had been playing with matches and all of a sudden one of them sparked, lighting the whole stack on fire.

"Why are you here?" I asked sharply.

My mom and dad looked at each other.

"You don't want me back," I said. "You don't want *me*. We talked about this over the phone."

"That's not true," Neil said. "Amir, look. I talked to your parents. They've assured me that they love you"—he turned to my mom and dad—"just the way you are. You have nothing to worry about."

I didn't believe it.

I leapt down from the bed, standing face-to-face with my family for the first time since the morning of graduation. Except that morning, they thought they knew who I was. Now they were staring at me like I was a stranger, looking me up and down in my boxers and white undershirt and messy bedhead.

I bolted past them and through the sliding glass door. Soraya tried to grab my arm, but I yanked it free. I ran down the stairs, but as I was rounding the corner to the second set of steps, I twisted my ankle and tumbled down five or six steps into the small grassy yard. I slammed my face into a clay flowerpot to the side of the stairs. I wanted to get back up, but my entire left side was throbbing.

"Amir!" I heard my mom's voice and her footsteps, rushing down the stairs. She knelt beside me. Her face was inches from mine, and she stroked my cheek like I was a little child.

"I can't go back," I sobbed. "I can't. I'm already here. And I can't go back. I can't go back. I can't go back."

I was shaking my head, my chest rising and falling sharply.

My mom just held me. She stroked my hair back. "Amir, we

want you back. Please, come home. It's okay. We love you. Please come home."

I saw my dad running down the stairs, three steps at a time, his face intensely focused as he brought my mom a wet cloth. My sister helped my mom clean up my cuts, wipe the soil off my cheeks. I tried to protest, but they wouldn't let me. I stopped talking, stopped whimpering, even, as I realized this: I was still their son. Their brother. Even knowing I was gay—even after I had exposed my whammies, even after the entire tally system broke down and there were no more points left, nothing else to score—they were still my family.

Interrogation Room 37

Amir

HOW AM I FEELING? *Nervous. Emotional. It's like I got swept up in a sandstorm yesterday and now I can't see clearly.*

I've had this terrible thought stuck in my head ever since the drive back to Rome with my family. It sounds awful to say it out loud, but . . . I didn't have to go with them. It all happened so quickly, and the fact that they flew all the way out to Italy—that meant something to me. So I went. But as we drove through the Italian countryside, I sat mostly silent in the back of the car with Soraya.

My mom did ask if I wanted to stop somewhere and change into clean clothes, and I said no. I'm sorry, sir. If I had known I was going to end up in here, talking to you for so long, I would have at least taken a shower.

Later That Day

WE ARRIVED IN Rome sometime in the afternoon to pack up my stuff. My apartment was on the fourth floor, the first one in a corridor just off the stairs. On the way up, Soraya wouldn't stop complaining about how hot it was. She was convinced the heat was going to damage her vocal cords. My mom commented that the flowers in the building's central courtyard were very pretty. My dad carried my duffel bag and said nothing.

When we reached my door, I let the key sit in the keyhole for a bit and closed my eyes. Then I pushed open the door.

Soraya stepped inside first. "This is where you've been living?" Her eyes darted around the single room, the small kitchen in the back, the unmade bed underneath the window.

"Yeah," I said.

She put one hand on her hip. "My dressing room is bigger than this."

"Soraya," my mom snapped.

"You don't have a dressing room," I said, giving her a look.

"Exactly," she said with a smirk. "How did you even afford this place?"

"Soraya! Eh!" my mom snapped again.

I resisted a smile. *You'd be surprised how many people are desperate for a Wikipedia page*, I wanted to tell my sister. Maybe another time. We had a lot of catching up to do.

My dad plopped down on the small futon next to the bed. "This is a nice apartment," he said, resting his arms behind his neck. "Much nicer than many of the apartments I lived in before I met your mom. She really whipped me into shape."

I glared at him. My mom cleared her throat awkwardly. "Let's pack up Amir's things," she announced.

I went and stuffed the rest of my clothes in my duffel and backpack. My parents started to pack up the pots and pans, but I told them they weren't mine, that the apartment had come furnished. My mom went to clean the bathroom, since she wanted to make herself useful, and since my landlady—an elderly artist who lived on the ground floor—had texted me on WhatsApp to leave the apartment *immacolato*. Spotless.

A minute later, my mom emerged from the bathroom holding a dull purple glow stick. "Amir, do you want this?"

I stared for a second, transported briefly back to Rigatteria, to Valerio. "Yeah, I'll take it." I stuffed the glow stick in my pocket.

I wasn't ready to pack up my things, much less leave Rome.

Our flight back wasn't until the next morning, and so my family wanted to go out for dinner. "Let's get pizza. We are in Italy! Take us to the most amazing pizza, Amir," my dad said in an overly cheerful tone.

We made our way over to a pizza restaurant that I knew had outdoor seating, just off of Piazza Testaccio. As we crossed through the park, the white marble fountain alive as ever, I imagined Jahan and his friends sprawled out on the benches, opening a bottle of prosecco, pouring it in plastic cups. My heart was thumping hard—at the possibility of running into one of Jahan's friends here, but also at the already distant memory of those afternoons.

What was the point of Rome without Jahan? It felt empty now.

My family and I were seated at a table on the sidewalk. The menu was long, and my parents asked the waiter a million questions—even after he had brought us English menus. Soraya and I rolled our eyes at each other like we always did when our parents embarrassed us like this. My sister looked really pretty with the wind blowing her hair, brown and shiny.

After we ordered, I went inside the restaurant to go to the bathroom. My mom gave my dad a look, her eyes wide and worried. "Seriously? Don't worry," I said. "I'm not going to run away again."

I weaved around the tightly packed tables inside and managed to ask one of the waiters in Italian where the bathroom was—*dov'è il bagno*. Thing is, I recognized that waiter right as the question came out of my mouth.

It was his lips. They deserved an exhibit of their own.

"Valerio?" I shook my head. "You work here?"

"Amir! Ay, I am sorry I have not texted. It was a busy weekend. I was working many shifts, and I thought I would see you at the Rigatteria party last weekend, but I did not, and I meant to text you, but—"

"It's okay," I said.

Valerio pulled me aside so another waiter could squeeze through. I flinched when he touched my arm. Valerio raised an eyebrow.

"Who are you here with?" he asked. "I cannot imagine it is a date, as you do not believe in mixing Italian food with romance."

I looked away and smiled. "That would be impractical."

"The mixing of foods, yes," Valerio said. "The date, it is all right. I would not be angry if you were here with someone else. You are an American in Rome. I imagine you are in very high demand."

I looked back at him. We stared at each other for a moment, Valerio and I. I was searching his face to see if he knew about Giovanni, how I had messed everything up, how nervous I was to be talking to him, but all I saw was the face of an Italian boy—those droopy eyes—endearingly cute and endearingly sweet.

"I'm here with my family," I finally said.

Valerio's face exploded. "What?"

"*Eccolo*," I said, and I pointed at them at the table outside.

"Wow. I am happy for you," Valerio said, squeezing my shoulder. "So they came around?"

I shrugged. "Maybe. We'll see."

Valerio's eyes fell to his feet. "So you are going back. To America."

"I am." I put my hands in my pockets and—oh my God. The glow stick.

Valerio must have seen me react, because he went, "I apologize, but I must ask: Is that a phone in your pocket or are you just happy to see me?"

"You did not just use that line."

"I have wanted to use that line for years! It is so American."

I took out the glow stick. Valerio gasped.

"No way!" he exclaimed. He took it from me and chuckled. "You are crazy."

"Maybe I am." I shook my head. "But you're crazier. You're the one who wanted to kiss at the Vatican."

"And I would do it again," Valerio said. He bit his lip and smiled. "I should get back to work. These pizzas are getting cold. But promise me something, Amir. Promise me that the boy I met at Rigatteria, the one I kissed behind the door at the Vatican, that he will not go anywhere. That he will stay right here"—Valerio tapped my heart—"whether other people approve or no."

I pulled in his hand and hugged Valerio tight. "Good luck with your mom," I whispered in his ear.

"Good luck with your family," Valerio said.

When I turned around, I noticed my family had been watching us.

After I went to the bathroom, I went back to our table outside, nearly knocking over a huge flowerpot on my way over.

"Who was that?" Soraya asked as I sat down.

"Who?"

"That guy you were talking to."

I glanced over at my parents. My mom's lips were a straight line. My dad's eyes flickered down to the table.

"Just a friend," I mumbled.

I hated myself as soon as that word left my mouth. *Friend.*

A moment passed. I felt like we were all holding our breath. "Rome is beautiful," my mom said, breaking the silence. "What have you seen here, Amir *joon*. The Colosseum?"

"No. I didn't see the Colosseum." The waiter arrived with our pizzas, and it was like we could all breathe again. Everyone dove in to grab a slice. "But I saw the Sistine Chapel."

"That must have been very nice," my mom said, cutting into her pizza with a fork and knife.

"Yeah, but it took a while to get there."

As we ate, I thought about the Sistine Chapel—how that Amir felt like another person ago, another eon ago. How that Amir would judge me hard for lying to my parents about my relationship with Valerio.

"Holy motherforking crap, this pizza is delicious," Soraya said, picking up a chunk of cheese that had fallen on the table and popping it in her mouth. My mom gave her a disapproving look. "What kind of cheese is this?"

"Gorgonzola," I said, and then I giggled. "Gorgonzooola," I said more slowly, gargling the word. "Gorgooonzzoollaaaa," I said a third time.

"Umm. Why are you saying 'gorgonzola' like that?" my sister asked.

I looked over my shoulder at the busy park, the marble fountain, the benches at the edge, and I turned back to Soraya.

"No reason," I said, smiling.

I took out my phone under the table and sent one last text from my Italian number.

Interrogation Room 38

Roya Azadi

WE WERE SO *happy to have Amir back.*

Interrogation Room 38

Soraya

IT WAS WEIRD *having Amir back.*

Something just felt different. It wasn't just that his hair was longer, curlier, or that he had a tan now and knew a bunch of Italian words. I don't know. He was just in his head a lot. It was like his mind was somewhere else. When we went out for dinner, Amir hardly looked at us. He just kept looking up at those pretty Italian buildings. It was the first time since the Instagram video that I realized he really did have a life there, in Italy, with friends.

Interrogation Room 37

Amir

THE INCIDENT ON *the plane. Right.*

I was sitting in an aisle seat, across from my family. I remember looking down the row, out the window, and there were little droplets in that airtight space.

Looking out that window, twisting my hands in my lap, I couldn't believe how quickly my life had changed. And not for the first time. Italy was already starting to feel like a fantasy I had made up.

Meanwhile, my family . . . they still didn't know who I was. All of a sudden, they were strangers to me.

I felt like a fraud. I couldn't get that line out of my head: Just a friend. I felt like I had made myself small. I had given in to my mom's tight lips, to my dad's flickering eyes. I despised them for being so uncomfortable at the sight of me talking to Valerio. I despised myself for giving in to their discomfort.

I looked over at them in their seats, my dad across the aisle, and I felt sad. They didn't know me. They didn't know this version of me, the me who had a crush on his tutor, who could give a speech in front of a group of weirdos and misfits, who could kiss a boy behind a door at the Vatican.

Maybe they never would. Maybe they didn't want to know that person.

As I chewed my gum, harder and harder, I realized there was only one way they could know that person. If I talked about it. I know my family—we're experts in avoidance. The apocalypse could happen and we would go about our day-to-day, pretending everything was fine. I practiced the words under my breath. "Mom and Dad . . . Mom, Dad . . . I want to talk . . . I want to talk about . . ."

Every breath made my mouth drier.

I took a short walk around the plane, up one aisle and down the other. I went the long way to the bathroom. I washed my hands, washed my face, dried my hands, dried my face. I came back to my seat.

I want to talk about the gay thing.

That stupid stereotype kept poking and prodding at my head. Iranian and gay: as incompatible as Amish people and Apple products.

That's when I spoke up: "I want to talk about the gay thing."

Interrogation Room 38

Soraya

I WAS TRYING *to sleep when Amir spoke up. Mom was sitting in the aisle seat, Dad was in the middle, and I was over at the end of the row, my head against the window. I was trying to get some rest before my performance, when I heard Amir go, "I want to talk about the gay thing."*

My eyes shot open. The plane was quiet and the cabin lights were dim. Amir was just standing there, in the aisle by Mom and Dad. He looked so nervous. I couldn't believe what he was doing. Other people around us were sleeping, too, and my mom asked him to lower his voice.

Interrogation Room 39

Afshin Azadi

IT WAS A *surprise. I will admit that. But Amir looked upset, and I told him, "Okay, baba jaan." That is a term of endearment in our language. He seemed upset, and I thought it might calm him down, and I said, "Okay, we can discuss it later."*

Interrogation Room 37

Amir

I SAID, "NO, *not later. Now." I looked over at my seat across the aisle from them. I didn't want to sit down. I knew that if I did, the minute I let myself get comfortable again, it would be game over.*

I didn't want to talk about it later. I knew myself; I knew that I would hide behind later.

It was like, I don't know, I was in control and not in control at the same time. Like an invisible hook was pulling me into this new place where I didn't want to be quiet. Not anymore. Not for one second longer.

Interrogation Room 38

Roya Azadi

IT WAS SO *public. People were sleeping. But Amir, he was insistent. His hands were shaking. He was saying, "No, not later. Now."*

I said, "Amir, please. Sit down and we will talk about this when we are home."

Interrogation Room 38

Soraya

THAT'S WHEN AMIR *said, "The whole reason I left home was because I was afraid to have this conversation. I'm not afraid anymore."*

Interrogation Room 39

Afshin Azadi

THE OTHER PASSENGERS *were staring. I wanted my family to be safe, and I knew how it must have looked for us to be raising our voices on an airplane. And so I tried comforting Amir. I tried rubbing his arm—*

Interrogation Room 38

Roya Azadi

AMIR KNOCKED HIS *arm back.*

Interrogation Room 37

Amir

IT WAS A REFLEX, *I think. I could tell my dad was just trying to keep the peace, put on a happy face. It didn't feel genuine.*

Interrogation Room 38

Roya Azadi

YOU HAD MENTIONED *someone who said they saw my husband and son get "violent" with each other. They were not violent. But it was enough for a woman in the row in front of us, a young white woman in a magenta athletic sweater, to get up and interfere. She got between Amir and my husband.*

Interrogation Room 38

Soraya

MY DAD AND *that woman got into an argument. She was really pushing his buttons, and I could see he was trying to control his temper. Other people started to turn around and watch.*

At one point my dad said something about Amir I really didn't like—I'm not going to repeat it—and that was when I got involved. I told Dad if he said that again, I wouldn't speak to him for the rest of my life. I'm pretty sure he was going to shut up after that, but that was when the flight attendants came and we got in trouble.

Interrogation Room 39

Afshin Azadi

THE WOMAN WAS *yelling at me. She was calling me backward.
She said some very unkind things about my religion. I tried my best to
stay calm, to ask her to please not interfere, because it was a family matter, and we would prefer to deal with our problems in private. But then
the woman said—*

Interrogation Room 37

Amir

"YOU THINK IT'S *a* problem *that he's gay?" She yelled this really loudly. Then Soraya started screaming at my dad. I guess maybe she actually believed he had said that, even though he hadn't. The woman had twisted his words. He definitely didn't say that. But it was too late.*

Interrogation Room 38

Roya Azadi

WHEN I SAW *the flight attendants rushing up the aisle, I had a terrible feeling in my throat. I knew that we would not be going home. Afshin had been stopped and interrogated before for much less. His history would not help us. I knew that we would have to explain ourselves in a room like this.*

Today

THE ROOM WAS cold and sterile, like a doctor's office. A Customs and Border Protection officer had escorted us past security, past the long lines and luggage carousels, and told us to sit and wait until our names were called. I was surprised to see so many other people in this waiting area: families, solo travelers, even a little boy who seemed to be by himself. Everyone looked nervous. Some of the families were chatting quietly.

When the officer walked away, Soraya took out her phone and started recording.

"Soraya, put that away," my mom said, swatting at her hand.

"This is unfair," Soraya said, yanking the phone away. She was recording a video. "What you see here is a Muslim family, being held against their own will—"

"Soraya!"

"Ma'am, you must turn off your cell phone in this room," barked a female officer standing against one of the walls.

My mom snatched the phone out of Soraya's hand and put it in her purse. She let out an exhausted sob.

"This is all my fault," I whispered. My mouth was dry. "I don't know what got into me. I just—"

"Amir, not now," my mom said.

Soraya rolled her eyes. "It's never a good time, is it?"

"Soraya—"

"Amir shouldn't have snapped on the airplane," Soraya said, cutting my mom off. "That was a mistake. But that was his *only* mistake. The *only* one."

Soraya glared at my parents. Then she reached over my mom and held my hand.

We sat there waiting for five, ten, fifteen minutes. My dad and I were sitting on opposite ends, with Soraya and my mom between us.

At the seventeen-minute mark, the officer announced she was leaving the room and that she'd be back momentarily. When she left, I heard my dad say something in a hushed tone. I thought he was talking to Soraya, but then she tapped my arm and he said it again.

"Two times two," he said.

I couldn't believe it. Multiplication tables. It's what we used to do when I was a kid at the doctor's office.

I shook my head.

"Two times two," he said again.

"Four."

"Three times three,"

"Nine."

But I didn't want to be that kid anymore. I didn't want to be my parents' baby forever, cute and innocent and harmless. I didn't want to be their toddler, the one who tripped and hiccupped and made everyone laugh.

I'm eighteen years old now. I'm practically an adult. I love my parents; I realize that now more than ever. I will always love them, and I will always be their son. But I have to be my own person, too.

"I'm sorry for overreacting on the plane," I said to my parents. "But I'm not sorry for who I am."

I turned to my dad, and while I know he'll deny it—he was born a Persian man and he will die a Persian man, a descendant of Xerxes and Cyrus the Great and other tough, impenetrable men—I swear, in that moment, tears welled up in his eyes. He bit his lip and sat quiet for a few seconds.

"Amir," he said.

The biggest lump formed in the back of my throat.

The female officer returned to the room, accompanied by another officer.

"Mr. Azadi," she said. My dad's face became serious again. "Please come with my colleague."

My dad got up and left. I heard my mom let out a deep breath, and then a minute later, they called my name, and I went.

Interrogation Room 37

Amir

MAYBE I'M EXPECTING *too much, too fast. Maybe it's a process. Soraya says they're doing better than most parents in their position. She says, "How many Iranian gay kids do you know whose parents are okay with it?"*

I get what she's talking about. I get that they're trying. But I also know they're struggling, and after the summer that I had in Rome, where I got to be me—all of me—it's hard for me to accept that it might take a while.

Interrogation Room 38

Soraya

WE CAN LEAVE *now?*

I think I get it. I get why my mom talks to you so seriously. You treat her differently. People like my mom have to be extra careful. You gave me that ice cream from the vending machine, and all you gave Mom were judgy looks.

Yes, I'm tired. Yes, I'm ready to leave. No, it's not because I miss Amir that much. Not after all the trouble he caused. It's because I have a dress rehearsal tonight, and there's no way I'm letting my understudy steal my part.

I guess I do miss Amir a little.

I don't care what my parents say or how long it takes them to accept Amir. I love him. We're a package deal. Our family isn't a family without him. I would say we're even better with him just the way he is. We're an even better family than we were before. This last month has been hard. The next month will probably be hard, too. But it's going to be the good kind of hard. The kind of hard that makes us better.

Now, can we go?

Interrogation Room 38

Roya Azadi

I WOULD LIKE to assure you that everything is fine in my family. My daughter, Soraya, she is a performer. Consider this one of her performances. She has another one coming up, this weekend. She is playing the very old, dramatic cat in Cats. The one with the solo that everyone loves. I think she will do a wonderful job.

Please, you don't have to apologize, Officer. Are you a mother? Yes? Then you understand where I am coming from when it comes to my children, my beautiful children, Soraya and Amir.

A mother's job is simple: it is to love her children, unconditionally. I am beginning to realize that from the moment my children were born, I have looked at them and loved them with certain conditions in mind.

It's time I change the way I look at the people I love. I'll admit that. It's time I look at Amir not with the weight of answers, but with the comfort of questions. Perhaps more of us should look at one another in that way.

A friend of mine with older children likes to say that at the beginning of your children's lives, you are teaching them. But there comes a point in life when they begin to teach you. I am starting to see that point. The ship is turning around. It will be a stormy ride, but we are going to make it through this journey together. All of us.

Interrogation Room 37

Amir

THAT'S ALL? YOU'RE *sure there isn't anything else you need?*

Thank you for returning my phone, sir. It looks like I have a couple of messages. Oh. A few of them are from Jahan. Voicemail. I don't think I can listen to these right now. I'll wait until I'm alone.

Can I tell you one last thing? One time in Rome, I was supposed to meet Jahan at Piazza Testaccio. Just the two of us. There was a performer in the square that day, a man in a fedora, who was playing pop songs on his violin. Soraya and I used to love listening to this string quartet on YouTube that played pop music, and I just immediately thought of her. This was right after she had told my parents that I was gay, and I knew she still felt awful about it. So I called her. Soraya picked up and said, "How many times can I tell you I'm sorry?" And I said, "Don't worry about it, just listen."

I kept Soraya on the phone for a while. I just wanted to listen with her. Eventually, I saw Jahan approaching, but I kept Soraya on the line until the very last second, when Jahan came up and put his hand on my shoulder and said "ciao," I hung up the phone a second later. But in that tiny moment, it was like my two worlds had merged.

That moment tasted sweeter than gelato.

In a perfect world, I would get two families. My Iranian family and my big, colorful gay one. I would get two communities. Two chances to be myself. My whole self. That should be the only number, the only score I have to keep. Two. It shouldn't have to look like a scoreboard. It should be simple.

Please don't get up, sir. I need more time. I need to put on a happy face before I see my family.

I need to breathe.

It is such a privilege, you know? To get to be yourself, all of yourself, in this great big world. To wear it like a tattoo, like all of Jahan's tattoos: permanent and out there for the whole world to see.

I'm tired of being quiet about who I am. Iranian people aren't quiet. We're storytellers. Jahan says we have a tradition of oral storytelling. That's what I've been doing in here, isn't it? Telling you my story. I may not be a brave hero like Rostam or a king like Cyrus, but damn it, talking to you today, telling you my story, is the most Iranian thing I've ever done.

I don't want to hide those parts of myself anymore. I want my family to see me. I want them to see me kissing Jackson in that car, blackmail be damned. I want them to see me riding on Valerio's motorcycle, dancing late into the night with Jahan and Neil at Rigatteria. I'm proud of that person. That person shouldn't be a stranger to them.

It's hard enough living one life; no one should have to go through the trouble of living two.

I'm guessing our time here is over, since you keep looking at the door.

Maybe that's the magic spell. Time. Maybe real problems aren't solved in those big fights, those loud moments, but in the time apart.

No, I don't need any more time. I'm ready. Let's go.

Soraya

MY PHONE! THANK YOU! *Ugh, I have so many texts. Madison really blew up my phone. She's so needy.*

Hey! Look, Mom, there's—

Afshin Azadi

AMIRI

Amir

Maman! Baba! Soraya!

Jahan

12:37 P.M.

CIAO, AMIR! CIAO from Cleveland. How are you? How is Rome? I heard you were going up to Neil and Francesco's mountain home—Franny was talking about it with someone the other night. Give them a big kiss for me.

I miss you, too. I love that you texted me that out of the blue. I miss you, and I miss Neil and Francesco, and I miss Rome.

I wish I'd gotten to say goodbye to you properly at my party the other night. I'm sorry if I seemed sort of cold or awkward. It was really sweet of you to come, and it was really not sweet of me to be in a bad mood. I had my weird reasons at the time. Anyway, it doesn't matter.

What matters is that you, sir, were a phenomenal friend this summer. I'll never forget when I first brought you to that dinner party. You remember? The one where you spilled all the meatballs? After you went to change your shirt, some snide asshole asked if you were going to be a liability, and Neil and I went *off* on him. *A liability? Che cazzo dici? What the fuck? That boy is our friend.*

And then you came back from Giovanni's room looking all spiffy in that soft blue shirt, and that was it. The rest of our summer was written.

We did have an incredible summer, didn't we? Yeah. We did. It was incredible. You were a gift to us this summer, really. Don't ever forget that. You are a fucking gift. People like you and me don't hear that enough.

Listen, I hope things get better with your family, Amir. If you ever want to talk about it, you call me. Seriously. I mean that now. I know family is important, and it's a process and all that, so I want you to know, I'm here for you, buddy.

Hey, remember those calculations you were going on about, that morning when I was being an ass? The "scoreboard" you were talking about? Look, you know I'm no math expert. But I can tell you this much: life is not a scoreboard, Amir. It is a big, beautiful, messy equation. One of those extra-complicated ones even a Nobel Prize–winning mathematician couldn't crack, let alone your poet friend who nearly flunked algebra.

One more thing, Amir. When you get back to Rome, I need you to do something. I left my bike parked on the street—by the shop outside my apartment, the one with all the trinkets in the window. That old thing got me everywhere. I bought it on my first day in Rome, and it's saved me more times than you can imagine. Just find a big pair of scissors, or a chainsaw or something, and cut the chain. It's yours.

ACKNOWLEDGMENTS

This book was partly inspired by the time I spent in Rome in the summer of 2018. Much like Amir, I had no idea when I landed that I would meet people who would change my life and become a special kind of family to me, if only for a short summer. Thank you to those people. You know who you are.

Thank you to my agent, Brooks Sherman, for caring about this book like it was your own baby. I know you have an *actual* baby now and he's absolutely adorable, but this book is pretty cute too, and that's all thanks to you.

To Roma Panganiban and everyone at Janklow & Nesbit, the best agency fam.

To Ken Wright, brave captain of the Viking ship, and the muscle behind all my books. To Kendra Levin, for your early support. To Maggie Rosenthal for truly bringing this book into the world. To Nancy Hinkel—petunia! Uranium! To Kaitlin Kneafsey for getting the word out like a pro. To Felicity Vallence, James Akinaka, Shannon Spann, Jen Loja, Maggie Edkins, Claire Tattersfield, Aneeka Kalia, and everyone at Penguin Young Readers, from the copy and production editors to all the incredible folks in marketing, sales, and school and library.

To the amazing team at Hot Key for their work on the UK edition, especially Emma Matthewson, Carla Hutchinson, and Lizz Skelly.

To Hellie Ogden, Emma Winter, Zoë Nelson, Ellis Hazelgrove, and Maimy Suleiman for your foreign rights wizardry.

To Adam Silvera, for listening to me babble for an hour on your rooftop about an idea for a story that I *had* to write. To Gayle Forman for a much-needed pep talk. To Lauryn Chamberlain for reading everything I write. To Nicole Bleuel for helping me gather my thoughts. To Patrice Caldwell for the "Has anyone actually read it yet?" moments. To Angie Thomas, Becky Albertalli, Adib Khorram, and Sara Farizan for your amazing blurbs. To all my friends for your support, especially my writing friends: Laura Sebastian, Mark Oshiro, Emily X.R. Pan, Cristina Arreola, Jeremy West, Jeffrey West, MJ Franklin, Dhonielle Clayton, Zoraida Córdova, and many more I'm sure I missed.

To Calvin Stowell for helping me get the Trevor Project scene right.

To the Trevor Project, for being such an important resource for queer teens. If you are a queer person struggling with suicidal thoughts or just want someone to talk to, please call the Trevor Lifeline at 1-866-488-7386.

To my readers: I feel honored and lucky to be able to write books for you. Stay different. Stay weird. And keep looking for your people—I promise it's worth the wait.

To all the librarians, teachers, and booksellers for doing the real work.

Finally, to Maman, Baba, Neeki, Arman, and Nava for filling my well with a lifetime of memories, support, and love.

ARVIN AHMADI

grew up outside Washington, DC. He graduated from Columbia University and has worked in the tech industry. When he's not reading or writing books, he can be found watching late-night talk show interviews and editing Wikipedia pages. He is also the author of *Down and Across* and *Girl Gone Viral*.